Children's Stories

Horacio A. Hernandez

DEDICATION:

For my beloved granddaughter, Nicole Samara
Ramkissoon.

Table of Contents

Children's Stories

(Note: The following stories are taken and adapted from the
Brothers Grimm Fairy Tales for all ages.)

INTRODUCTION

This anthology is a panoramic view of all my children's stories, written at different times and on different themes and genres. Among the themes, there is a wide range of stories about love, death, life, life after death, courage, innocence, envy, etc. Among the genres, there are tales that are realistic, surrealistic, fantastic, popular, etc. Some of these tales fit very well with the narrative technique of magical realism; others are based on folklore, beliefs and superstitions, myths, and religious beliefs. There are allegorical tales and historical fiction. Some of these stories were taken and adapted from my book of stories for adults. But, for the most part, these stories are based on my own experience, on events and situations I have observed throughout my life, as I have found myself in different places and circumstances.

I should mention here that some of these stories have their origin in a dream or revelation I had at a very young age. For example, "The boy who became an angel" reveals the strong emotion I felt and the worry of having to reveal to my family and others when my wings began to grow, and how I had to hide or disguise with my clothes the promontories of the wings when they began to grow.

On the other hand, it is remarkable the marked realism of some of the stories, as in "The mother hen", which is a product of my experience as a farmer while living with my parents, and "Poverty", which expresses the harshness of life in the countryside, especially in times of drought, famine, and economic precariousness. But also, I must say that these were the best moments of my life while living with my parents. These are all real, well-lived experiences.

Chapter 1

The mother hen

Animals, like some marginalized human groups, often need a spokesperson—someone to speak for them and express their complaints and sorrows to the world since humans do not understand their language or their way of communicating. Here is a typical example among domestic birds. It is a hen.

Clo, clo, clooo! Co-co-te-co! For those human beings who think that we, hens, don't think, let me tell you just one episode of my life. Clo, clo, clooo! Co-co-te-co! Once upon a time, due to humans' appalling behavior of annihilating our species because of their daily consumption habits, I made the decision to lay my eggs far from the house and away from the chicken coop so that people could not eat them daily and I would not be forced, once again, to wait for another season of the year to realize my dream of being having my own chicks, to raise them with love and protect them from all evil, as my ancestors taught me.

So, the decision was made. Every day, I would go to my secret nest to lay my egg. But the problem was that one day, the owner heard that I was happy. I had just laid my egg when he heard my: Clo, clo, clo, clooo! Co-co-te-co! Upon hearing me, he exclaimed, "That hen is dropping her eggs. Listen to how she comes clucking; it seems she has just laid her egg." Notice how he accuses me of "dropping the eggs" simply because I was not making them available to him. He then went around the area where I came from, looking for my nest to see if he could find it. But it was all in vain. I had calculated a strategic and hidden place far away from the house.

Because he couldn't find my eggs, one day, when I came very hungry to eat the corn kernels he was throwing to the other animals, he caught me and tied me up for twenty-four hours so that the next day, he could chase me when I had to rush desperately to lay my egg. Clo, clo, clo, clooo! Co-co-te-co!

That day, when my master tied me up by one leg, I was so angry that I wanted to show him that I was smarter than him and that I was determined not to reveal the location of my nest. I was sure that the only thing he wanted was to take all my eggs to satisfy his usual consumption habits, denying me the opportunity to raise my first set of chicks.

You don't want to know the satisfaction I felt when I managed to outwit him and rush towards my nest. What happened was that when I was running like crazy to my nest, I noticed that he was chasing me because, as I told you before, his only intention was to find out where I was hiding my eggs. So, every time I ran in the direction of my nest, I saw him running too.

I then decided to come up with a strategy: I pretended that I could not find my nest; as I approached the specific place where I had laid my eggs, I stopped several times as he watched me and ran from one place to another to confuse him. At this point, I was desperate to lay my egg because the master had tied me up for a few hours, and the precise time to lay my egg had already passed.

Finally, during one of those stops, I waited for that precise moment when he got distracted looking elsewhere, and I quickly slipped away from his presence and rushed to the place where I had my hidden nest. Finally, I managed to lay my egg, and, this time, I did not make any noise—I didn't sing my chicken egg song, so he would not discover my secret place.

Forgive me for saying "Cocoteco!" because that comes naturally to me; it is our way of expressing joy for having laid an egg, a potential future son or daughter. But this time, for obvious reasons, I restrained myself from squawking so as not to be discovered by my master.

However, I must add here that since I did not live in a pen or chicken coop, the condition of living in an open place provided the environment for me to escape from my master. Evidently, I was not a poultry, and I lived openly in harmony and in direct contact with nature, so I raised my chicks.

Now, returning to this episode of my life. I want to point out that you can't imagine how happy my owner was when he saw me returning with all my chicks, seeing them as future prey for his feeding habits. However, what he never suspected was that I had educated my chicks so that they could escape from their master when they reached adulthood. The first warning I gave them when they reached the weight of a pound was not to let themselves be attracted by two or three grains of corn that the master throws at them so that they begin to be suspicious of everyone so as not to fall, unexpectedly, into the master's pot, etc. Clo, clo, clo, clooo! Co-co-te-co!

On the other hand, I must mention here the tastelessness and suffocation I had to go through day and night while I was heating my eggs for almost three weeks—to be more precise, it was two weeks, four days, twenty hours, fifty-nine minutes, and fifty-nine seconds. On a regular basis, I would always get nervous when I felt the sound of an animal approaching my nest, especially if I suspected it was an egg-loving dog or a wild ferret. Most of the time, when a can-turning dog approached me, giving it a single peck was enough to make it flee from my presence, but when it was a wild ferret, they were more violent; I had to attack them with a blow of my beak and claws to make them leave my nest. Other times, the noise I heard was the snorting of a horse or the wandering of a cow that happened to pass by the place while eating some fresh grass. I enjoyed the sunny days and would constantly thank God that it was not the rainy season, as I sometimes had no choice but to endure the heavy downpours. Clo, clo, clo, clooo! Co-co-te-co!

On the other hand, what made me take this decision to act defensively towards my master was the fact that he had taken all my eggs, and since I insisted on staying in my nest, even though I had no eggs to incubate because of my maternal instinct, he came up with the idea of putting duck eggs in my nest, especially from ducks that did not like to stay in the nest. This made me stay in my nest for four weeks—one week longer than the time required to incubate my chicks.

But really, you cannot imagine all the pains I had to go through to raise my new chicks. For example, the first big surprise I had was seeing that all my offspring came out with wide and half-flattened beaks. Added to this misfortune were all those anxious moments I had to endure when I saw my chicks persistently getting into the water. When I called them insistently, they usually came; however, other times, they preferred to stay where they were because, on some occasions, I called them even though I didn't have food for them; they'd come to realize it was just an excuse to get them out of the water. Also, I know that they wanted me to accompany them in the water, but I could not swim; sometimes, I would please them by getting to the edge of the pond until the water reached the level of my feathers, but I would immediately get out of the water for fear of drowning. Clo, clo, clo, clooo! Co-co-te-co!

Back to the secret plan I had devised to educate my children on how to protect themselves from the master and his people and avoid being caught to be used as culinary delights. At this point, all my young ones had reached an average weight of one or one and a half pounds after a few days of rain and were able to fly. As they were always around the house, they heard rumors that the master and his family had invited their friends to come over for a feast, which would include a big pot of stew with some of my children. So it was that at dawn the next day, very early in the morning, they all gathered and took flight like eagles, disappearing into the air, never to return. The good thing was that I had already prepared them to live on their own when the time came. That same morning, I, too, took advantage of the first rays of sunshine of that clear and clean day, climbed up to the roof of the house

to ruffle my feathers for a few minutes, and fearing
that perhaps the master might use some revenge
against me, I took flight and flew away in search of
new horizons.

Clo, clo, clo, clooo! Co-co-te-co!

Chapter 2

Animals that can predict human death.

A certain parish priest of a community, which he loved very much, came up with a brilliant idea. He noticed how people suffered when they saw their loved ones die and, above all, the degree of despair they fell into when the death of a loved one caught them by surprise. That's why one day he thought to himself, "Well, if God would give me the opportunity to at least recognize a few days in advance when a person was going to die, I could announce it to their relatives in advance and then the family would have the necessary margin of time to plan, within their possibilities, everything concerning the funeral of their loved one.

God, seeing the priest's good intentions, granted him that opportunity. One night while he was sleeping, God gave him a revelation and said to him, "When you go to visit the sick ones in the hospital, take one of your pets with you, and watch the pet's movements; it will give you some sign of which one will be the next person to die. Each time, take a different one." Then, upon awakening the next morning, the priest was very jubilant because he knew God had spoken to him, and he could remember all the details of his revelation. As he got up, he said these words, "Thank you, Lord! So be it!"

When it came to the elderly, the priest was more concerned that they were well-prepared for their final journey to the afterlife. That is why he almost always frequented the local hospital to prepare the elderly, who were very sick, to start straightening the path that would lead them directly to their Creator.

Thus, we see how the priest made use of certain resources offered to him by nature and revealed to him by God to achieve his goals. He had three pets: a black and white cat, a lizard, and a parakeet, which the children loved to come to his house to see and feed. This was a good idea, as the priest often did not have the financial means to feed these animals himself.

The mysterious thing about these little animals was that they had the power to predict the death of a human being. That is why, when he went to the hospital for his routine visits, he was usually accompanied by one of them. However, the priest did not want the people of the community to realize so that they would not be frightened when they saw him making visits with one of his pets. Whenever he was accompanied by the cat, he would notice how the cat would walk among the sick, and when he recognized the one who was going to die soon, he would lie down briefly next to the old man or woman, and immediately, the father would go to that person and make the necessary preparations for their good death:

> Purgatorium anima, tibi solum peccati mundi, conjurote in nomine Patris, et Filii, et Spiritus Sancti. Amen.

As soon as he finished his ritual, he would run to call the nurse to notify the relatives of the next dying person, giving them enough time to prepare for the funeral they would soon be hosting. No one had the slightest idea how these little animals helped him identify the next dying person, as he alternated his visits with a different one each time. Nor could anyone notice the preparation he made for the person, as he did it in Latin, and sometimes he prayed with more than one person at a time, but in a different way from the one whose turn was not yet due.

On days when the priest would visit these elders with his lizard, he would watch the lizard wander among them before stopping momentarily in front of one of them. The priest also noticed how the lizard's skin would change color for an instant. So even if he was talking with one of the other elders, he didn't take his eyes off his pet until he caught the signal that would tell him who would be the next to embark on the eternal journey. In a sly manner, he would then proceed to give the proper instructions for the family to prepare for the funeral.

Finally, when he visited with his parakeet, he would watch the parakeet fly from one side of the room to the other. However, if he saw the little bird fly three consecutive times over one of the elderly, he would immediately approach him to face the soul of the next dying person. Then, he would ask the nurse to urgently notify the family of their loved one's funeral arrangements.

Purgatorium anima, tibi solum peccati mundi, conjuro te in nomine Patris, et Filii, et Spiritus Sancti. Amen.

After praying for the person, he would return home to rest and meditate on what had happened and how God was using these little animals to help families prepare for what would be their last responsibilities to their loved ones in this life. Finally, he would proceed to prepare the church for the services and eulogy he would have to give in front of the family and friends of the soon-to-be deceased. With these ideas in mind, the priest would immediately call the church altar server and the volunteer who would oversee decorating the church for the occasion of the funeral.

The predictive faculty of these little animals and birds were so effective that they hardly made a mistake in choosing the right person. On one occasion, when the priest was on his usual visit to the hospital with his parakeet, something strange happened, leading the priest to believe that his pets had made a mistake when, in fact, it was a perception error on the part of the priest himself—as his pets were never wrong in their choosing of the person who was going to die next.

Well, what happened was that while the priest was visiting one of the hospital wards, the mayor of the community, who had decided to visit a friend of his who was ill, arrived. Suddenly, the priest noticed that instead of making the signal on one of the sick elders, the parakeet hovered around the mayor. Well, the priest, believing that it was a mistake, did not take any action to warn the nurse like he usually did.

However, as the priest made his way out of the hospital, he saw something that caught his attention: a crowd of people and police rushing in all directions and in confusion. Upon getting to the scene, he learned that the mayor had passed away. According to some witnesses, two individuals on a motorcycle, supposedly the mayor's enemies, had approached him and shot him at close range before speeding away; the mayor was unable to defend himself.

Chapter 3

The legend of the three crowned doves

According to the engravings in a cave near the coast southwest of the Gulf of Arrows, which the natives call the Haitises, there lived an indigenous princess whom many considered to be a *ciguapa*. The *ciguapa* was a mysterious being that had magical powers, which allowed it to change its physical appearance and walk backwards with its feet twisted in that direction. People were very afraid of it, especially children. This place had been far from the reach of our conquerors, so the natives used it as their natural refuge. They spent a long time there without being discovered. The beauty of this place was like a scene from a movie—the rocky and flowery keys gave the impression that they were walking through the gulf, the flock of birds clouded the sky, the forest was dazzling, and the waves of the sea penetrated through the interior of other arched caves that looked like small temples.

The indigenous narrator who told me the story said that this indigenous princess, accompanied by her handmaids, lived in the Haitises cave for a long time without having been discovered by other indigenous groups or the first Spaniards who sighted them there. For this reason, the first time someone noticed the presence of the indigenous princess in that place, they thought she was a *ciguapa*.

At one end of the cave, there was a precipice or abyss that led to a subway river that, according to some more recent explorers, flows into the sea. According to the account of the *cacique* who told us about it, this indigenous princess lived in the cave with two of her servants. It is also said that when the first Spanish defeated them in their own territory, instead of surrendering, they threw themselves into the abyss. The explorers searched for them on the side of the precipice, but they could not find them anywhere.

The indigenous woman's account states that when the explorers approached the abyss into which the indigenous had thrown themselves, they saw three little crowned doves fluttering over their heads, trying desperately to get out of the cave. The explorers understood that they were either the souls of the three missing indigenous or some mysterious transformation of the indigenous.

Because of this, from that time until today, every visitor who passes by the cave claims to have seen the three doves coming out of it. This legend gave origin to the name of the crowned doves that appear in that place, as these doves have a white crown on their heads, like the white feather crowns worn by the indigenous princess and her handmaids.

Chapter 4

The strange
relationship between
the cat and the mouse

(A fable)

This story is about how two traditional enemies begin a mutual relationship based on friendship and the practice of love. First, we will comment on the initial lives of Mr. Cat and Mr. Mouse as common beings of their species and how the meeting between Mr. Cat and Mr. Mouse happened.

Well, Mr. Mouse was tired of constantly having to dodge Mr. Cat's lurks; it had even cost him the lives of some of his relatives. Until one day, he began to reflect on his natural wisdom and on how to put an end to the bad habits of a cat who did not even behave like other cats as a result of being infected by the bad behavior of some of the human beings with whom he lived. His contact with humans made him lose his natural tactics, and for that reason, he acted clumsily in a natural environment. Despite this, the cat had learned the language of humans.

Meanwhile, the strategy that Mr. Mouse decided to put into practice was to steal meat from a butcher's shop and fish from a fish market so that every time he saw the cat, he would throw him a piece of meat or fish. This way, the cat would begin to change his attitude toward the mouse. Eventually, a philosophical meeting with Mr. Cat took place, which was long awaited by Mr. Mouse. This meeting began with some well-planned philosophical questions from Mr. Mouse:

"What great harm have I done you to make my life, as well as that of my kind, so miserable? Have we caused you great harm by only wanting to live freely in the same environment you enjoy? Why don't you stop your persecution and let us live in communion so that we can better cope with this life so full of confusion?"

"Well, well, Mr. Rat, what eloquent questions! I've never thought about why I behave the way I do, but before I give you an answer, could you explain to me what you mean when you say that this life is full of confusion?"

"Well, Mr. Cat, don't you find it confusing and contradictory what humans do with many individuals of our species? On one hand, they elevate us to the category of prince and princess for their amusement and enrichment, as they do in the world of Disney, while on the other hand, thousands of products are invented with the intention of eliminating all individuals of our species, such as rat poisons, mechanical traps, DDT, which produce other evils that threaten the whole civilization and pollute our water bodies."

As proof of his complaint or lament about humans, Mr. Rat explained to the cat that it would be enough for him to make an appearance in front of a maid or lady of the palace when he goes in search of his food for the said lady to scream to the sky or fall kicking to the floor, causing such commotion and confusion that even the palace guard is put into action in our pursuit. Suddenly the screams of some lady of palace are heard:

"Oh, look at a mouse! I'm dying! Help! Help!" Screams the plump maid until she falls unconscious on the floor as if someone had killed her.

"Also, I remember that, on one occasion, after hearing the lady's scream, I ran away and took refuge inside a shoe that turned out to belong to the master of the house. I don't want to remember the events of that day in which I lost a piece of my tail."

"And how did such unpleasant misfortune befall you?" asked Mr. Cat.

Well, that gentleman, like a clumsy, chubby giant, when he got out of bed and put on his shoes, gave me a tremendous stomp that, if it hadn't been for a certain bite I gave him on the foot, I wouldn't be telling about it now. Those ill-tempered giants are not content only with physical violence, but even with their slander and blasphemies, they cause us great harm. Among the many evils of which they accuse us, they say that we were the cause of the bubonic plague of yesteryear. They never look at the good that we, as environmental controllers, have done.

Likewise, we must also admit that there are some positive things that the mouse learned from Mr. Cat and his relationships with human beings. Well, Mr.

Cat, after listening to Mr. Mouse's long complaint, meditated for a great while, and after much reflection, he came to the conclusion that the only sublime thing he had learned from his relations with human beings was that they spoke of a "Redeemer" and that this Redeemer "would take us to a place where there is plenty of meat and fresh fruits with which we can live all our lives without having to destroy one another." That is why Mr. Cat understood that, beyond all those beings, there was a superior being who maintained the harmony of his own existence and of all that existed.

It was then that he decided to answer Mr. Mouse the next time he met him.

"Well, you are right, Don Rata. I seem to be an ungrateful person for never having paid attention to the evil I caused others. I beg you, with all my heart, to forgive the unreason by which my life was guided. Forgive the bad habits I inherited. Well, I didn't know that with my bad actions, I was hurting others." And so, Mr. Cat continued giving him millions of excuses to try to alleviate the many evils that his feline actions had caused to other beings.

"I don't even live for myself anymore," says Mr. Mouse, "but for my children, especially for my last son, Miguelito, who was recently born to me."

While Mr. Cat listened to him attentively, the depth of his message and the sobriety of his expression made it seem to him as if he were in the presence of an angel.

"Therefore, Mr. Cat, I invite you to a solid and fraternal relationship, in which lies the future of our existence," Mr. Mouse concluded.

"Oh, a friend of mine, Mr. Mouse," replied Mr. Cat after listening to his eloquent exposition and invitation, "don't think that living among these people has been all glory. If I have survived at all, it is because I am an intelligent creature."

Then, he began to explain his existential problems as a feline being. That is, his life as a cat. For example, he tells him about his seven lives, as people invent them to make his own existence harder, etc.

"Well, you see, Mr. Cat, in my case, there is nothing that bothers me more than hearing people say that because one mouse ate the cheese, all the mice ate it because not all mice have the same intentions."

"So, as I was saying, Mr. Mouse, those people use us as an excuse to insult their female companion. They attribute to us having said that when we get up, we cross ourselves, saying, 'Things misplaced, careless woman.'

And, as if that were not enough, sometimes, I have felt 'like a cat in hot zinc' because for walking in the wrong places, they have even thrown hot water on me with the intention of killing me. Other times, I have dreamed that I have lived in foreign lands where cats are treated better than people. Well, they use us as pets, and they even give us nannies; for our ailments, doctors; and they even take us to the pedicure."

"Oh, don't pay attention to those treacherous people since that is nothing more than a dream for those who are waiting in this life."

This is how the dialogue between Mr. Cat and Body Mouse continued; they became so close that he baptized his son, Miguelito. However, amid this conversation, there was some confusion. But Mr. Cat reflected on all that Mr. Mouse had said, and he was so moved that his heart was softened; his emotion was so great that he threw himself on Mr. Mouse, hugged him, and gave him a tremendous squeeze. The mouse was so frightened that, amid such confusion, all he could think in that moment was: "Oh, I don't care who eats whom anymore." Well, despite all that, from that moment on, they lived happily with each other, in full communion, and from generation to generation.

Chapter 5

The museum of the mysterious doll

The Swannanoa Valley is home to a community of the same name, a picturesque community nestled in the southwestern part of North Carolina. The breathtaking panorama of the gently rolling Appalachian Mountains at the foot of lakes, waterfalls, and streams presents the spectacle of a vast natural park.

The mountains of Swannanoa dress up with the passing of the seasons; during the spring, the forest exhibits a characteristic green color of chromatic shades in the exuberance and transparency of its foliage. From there, spring, like the magic of nature, creates the different fountains and waterfalls of crystalline waters that feed the prairies and their inhabitants. In some places, the mountains are so high that they seem to touch the sky and so close that it seemed like one could touch them with his hands. The trees give the impression of speaking to any visitor who approaches them.

The houses are scattered through the trees. From time to time, some young girls are seen trotting, as if they were nymphs, along the small roads, hiding among the trees, as if they were trying to escape the satirical looks of the few drivers who pass by.

Among the many attractions in the Swannanoa Mountains is a small museum. Every American tourist or foreigner, who wanders through this community on the way to Black Mountain, North Carolina, considers a visit to this small museum known as "The Mystery Doll Museum" a must. As you approach this place, it gives the impression of a normal residence. However, as soon as you step over the threshold of the front door, your gaze is captivated by the presence of a large, human-sized doll that appears to be alive.

As a spectator, the closer you get to the doll, the more you become aware of the details of that mysterious object. Your heart seems to beat faster and you're left almost breathless as you learn how that doll came to become the mysterious object that it is. No less impressive is the whole residence full of tiny beings of all sizes, kinds, colors, materials, and much more. The varieties range from porcelain dolls, rag dolls, stuffed dolls, plastic dolls, metal dolls, and wooden dolls to dolls made of whatever materials the manufacturer of all these bright and multicolored things could think of.

Every room in that strange residence looks like an expert collector's display. But the point where you are almost breathless is when you finish reading the written message found in a centuries-old-looking manuscript, covered by a dark glass and frame, a bit stained by time. As soon as you are halfway through the manuscript, you feel all the hairs on your body stand on end; the first thing that crosses your mind is whether you should continue reading what you are reading or if you should stop at that moment and leave that half haunted or enchanted place that leaves every spectator speechless as if it were a horror scene.

The fact is that, from the reading of the manuscript and the details offered by the guides and guardians of that place, one learns that that doll was a normal person made of flesh and blood like you and me. It was a young Dominican girl who had been born and raised on the Samana Peninsula in the Dominican Republic, part of one of the largest islands in the Caribbean Sea. Since colonial times, that place has been contaminated by the practices of *Santería* and voodoo. The only thing that is known about that girl is that she was the spoiled child of a rich family and that she was fascinated by dolls.

Some dared to say that when a doll fell into her hands, it seemed to come to life and that she was seen playing with the other dolls as if they were a set of miniature living beings. In unclear circumstances, this girl, at a very young age, moved to North Carolina, where it is believed that she obtained her basic studies, although no specific evidence has been found so far.

The inhabitants of Black Mountain claim that this young woman lived for a long time in the same house that is now used as the museum. Others say that she was married for some time, but no one could say for sure if they had children or not. What everyone seems to agree on is that the young wife was fond of dolls and that she used to collect them of all types, sizes, colors, materials, etc. Many inhabitants of that place give testimony to having seen her on certain occasions in some flea markets, not only in that place but also in places as far away as Santo Domingo, Puerto Rico, Massachusetts, Albany, Buffalo, New York, and North Carolina.

What boggled everyone was how all that spectacle came to be, why there were no objects other than dolls in that residence, and what happened to all the other normal objects in that residence. However, as you visit each room and observe every detail of that immense puzzle, the story of that mysterious couple begins to emerge. You soon learn that the lady's husband, despite living almost all his life surrounded by these tiny beings, ended up hating dolls because the wife, as she bought a new collection of dolls, had to use the space occupied by her husband's things to store her dolls.

What once started out as simple household ornaments grew into small colonies of tiny creatures representing all the species of nature. All the main seats were occupied by the collection of bears, which stretched from the living room to the bathroom. One whole room was occupied by different models of elephants; another by little houses of different sizes; and the kitchen was occupied by the representation of every domestic animal, from the rooster to the rabbit, as if it were a farmyard. In the corridor, one could stumble upon a deer. Some claim to have heard the husband complain about the wife because she had filled her closets and replaced some of her books on the shelves with new collections of dolls.

As time went on, she packed her husband's books, clothes, and other equipment into boxes and moved them to a large storage room at the back of the house. Whenever the husband left for work or was absent for a short time, as required by his duties, he would return home to find what had become a nightmare for him. When he was absent for a week, he would return to find almost his entire office occupied by those tiny beings he hated so much.

"But this is the last straw," he expressed very irritated one day. "This is going to drive me crazy; I have to do something about this woman." At that moment, the wife, who knew very well what the husband's intention was, began to make her own. Before the husband's astonished eyes, she began to turn everything she touched with her hands into a doll: the husband's professional books, the valuable office objects, the photos of his mother and grandparents, and many others. Suddenly, the husband, in desperation, threw himself on her to stop her, and when she touched him, he too was turned into a large doll. This is the second large doll that is located on the threshold of the door. That explains the doll's strange, frizzled expression, which seems to tell us something or to want to explain its misfortune when we see it. The strange thing is that she herself could not escape the spell, being converted into that big doll located at the entrance of the small museum, which attracts the attention of visitors.

In the end, the inhabitants of that place in the Black Mountains of North Carolina decided to preserve for posterity as a museum the living history of that strange couple and their mysterious disappearance. (Oct. 15, 03)

Chapter 6

Lucia's vision of glory

(Character from *The Amazing Wedding, Oct. 30, 2011, 9:20 p.m.*)

I wonder, O death, where is your sting? For all evil, sorrow, grief, suffering, tears, pain, and evil thoughts are now a thing of the past. If at times, some brief remembrances come to mind, it is only to prove the grace and mercy in which we find ourselves. Here everything is joy and perpetual life. Well, did the wise Christians say that glory was something we could not even imagine? These are new heavens and new earths that are like nothing we have ever seen.

We are surrounded by angels everywhere. They are our guides and protectors wherever we go. Because there are so many of us, they don't want anyone to be hurt by the excitement in which we find ourselves amidst so much joy, jubilation, and happiness. It all comes to us from Him, our Great God and Heavenly Father. We are all surrounded by a resplendent aurora, a kind of radiant yet transparent rainbow that permanently guides us toward Him. We are in a constant becoming; it is as if it were one of those great religious festivals we used to have on earth.

Music comes to us from everywhere. Sometimes we are surrounded by a host of angels singing. Other times, we are surrounded by flocks of birds of all sizes and colors. There is something unseen in these birds; they are not like the ones we had on earth. These birds, of all shapes and colors, not only fly the normal way but also upside down. They move in small circles and radiate lights and by the sweet melodies of their trills that permeate the place, they too show us their jubilation. It is as if they were putting on a show around us to entertain and cheer us with their charm and kaleidoscopic fluttering. It seems as if we were in the presence of a magical or enchanted landscape, but those are words of the earth that fall short of expressing all the grandeur of what we see.

Everyone here is an Ah! Oh! Wow! It's incredible every time we fix our gaze on any detail. But these exclamatory words come to us from our memory of earth. They cannot capture the full magnitude of what we constantly see, hear, or feel around us. I feel that we have developed other kinds of senses that we didn't even know we had. It's as if we can see with our ears and even through our skin. If we approach a rose in this natural and celestial landscape, it is another spectacle; if we touch it, it is transformed into bouquets of roses of all colors and aromas that cause us ecstasy and joy, a synesthesia of sublime perceptions. The most pleasant surprise is that our Savior has given us the ability to create the things that we like around us in this enchanting landscape. What a joy it is to see all these new and enchanting things spring forth to life and become the product of our imagination!

If we focus on the animals we see, we notice that sheep and woolly deer of all colors and sizes abound, as well as some species never seen before. They are all part of this enchanting and sublime environment in which we find ourselves. In this constant becoming towards our Heavenly Father, we move as if we were flying. In this aurora of enchantment that envelops us, we are guided by multicolored rays that are pleasing to our sight and other senses that we are gradually developing. It is through this resplendent aurora that our physical and spiritual sustenance comes to us.

The definition of manna from the earth, the nectars of flowers, and royal jelly fall short of the taste and pleasure we experience; it's as if we were ingesting honey, vegetables, and fruits through our heavenly veins without having to eat them. These luminous rays that come to us from our Heavenly Father provide us with all that our new body needs to extend our life forever.

On earth, we were never told of a constantly smiling, joyful, and attentive Jesus like the one we see beside our Heavenly Father. We see him seated at his throne of precious stones, surrounded by angels and archangels who constantly serve them and by the multitudes of us who constantly approach him. It is as if he is engaged in an endless dialogue with those who approach them, to whom he looks and smiles, wrapped in a cascade of laughter with those who pass around him.

As we approach the father or the Son, the ecstasy and pleasure we feel have no measure or comparison; we perceive everything with our new senses, which we do not even know how they work with such accuracy and enchantment that they keep us perplexed and joyful at every instant. The Scriptures clearly stated that the light of the sun, moon, and stars was no longer required, but everything appeared to exist in some other dimension. It seems that all those stars that we saw before are overshadowed by the great radiance, lights, and luminous rays that come to us from our Heavenly Father and penetrate all this enchanting world, which extends far beyond what our eyes and the new senses that we possess can perceive. This light is far brighter than the noonday light of any summer day of splendor on earth.

These moments of remembrance of the earth come to us in fractions of a second and at any time, just so we can witness the grandeur and magnitude of what we see here and understand that this light is eternal. Here, there is no darkness like in the physical world in which we used to live, where darkness was part of the game and movement of the stars in their past creation.

But we may wonder: where are our loved ones? What happened to them? Well, of course, they are all here; they are part of these great multitudes that are constantly approaching our Creator and

Redeemer. Sometimes we meet our children, siblings, parents, grandparents, great-grandparents, and great-great-grandparents whom we had never seen before; they all come to meet us, joyful, shining, smiling, and they hug and kiss us. Then, we move on, sometimes together, sometimes apart. The new encounters are constant and endless. We could never have imagined such things.

Why is the sunlight and the light of the other stars that we used to know not needed here? Because here, there is true light, splendor, brightness, eternal warmth, joy, enchantment, music, and eternal landscapes, as well as a serene peace that penetrates us to the depths of our souls. Now the light is in each one of us and in all the beings that surround us. The movement of the celestial birds, angels, and other beings that move around us light the multicolored sky like the fireworks that we used to see on earth during holidays; but instead of noises, what we perceive are pleasant songs and praises to our Great King, the sound of trumpets, harps and other instruments sweeter and more pleasant to our senses, which we do not know how to describe. All these beings are our radiant suns and stars that emanate and radiate the light and splendor that we receive from our Creator and Redeemer. To Him be honor and glory, Alleluia! Holy, holy, holy! Amen!

That lowly dust of which the poets on earth spoke has been transformed into living and illuminated dust. They too are part of the praises, applause and cheers for our Creator and Redeemer Alleluia!

Moreover, it is beautiful to see husbands and wives who are the products of innocent love relationships that never came to fruition on earth, and here they became a reality, all within this new eternal spiritual dimension. Love has triumphed! Hallelujah! And the angels sing praises to our Eternal Savior and Redeemer!
Amen!

Chapter 7

The wise Taino

A major difference between Columbus' original diary and the version of the diary collected by Father Bartolomé de las Casas is the story of the indigenous priest, known rather as "The wise Taíno." This priest could predict so much about the future that even the Spaniards took him seriously because he once predicted the great plague of ants that would appear in the north of the island, which made them move the capital of the first European colony of the American Continent to the southern part of the Spanish island. This fact can be verified in the history of the first Spanish island in the Caribbean, known as Hispaniola.

During that same period, when the construction of Fort Christmas, the first Spanish fortress on the island, was barely known, the Taino Sage also predicted that the Spaniards would make many vertical constructions, that there would be flying chariots, like big birds, that would fly through the clouds; and that they would be able to reach the moon. It was well understood that he was referring to some kind of ship of the future because, although he used the phrase "flying horses like birds" and was asked to draw what those flying birds would be like, he drew giant horses with their riders and, instead of legs, he drew two circles on each side of the horses, which seemed to the Spaniards to be some kind of chariots with wheels.

The diary also specifies that the Taino sage was one of the advisors of Cacique Guacanagarix and that the Spaniards took him seriously, not only because he predicted the plague that caused the first capital of the colony to change its location but also because he foretold that in the future a wave would rise from the sea that would cause a lot of damage to the populations near the beach. This great wave is what is known in modern times as a tsunami. The first tsunami, which is recorded in the history of Dolorosa Village, and which produced many victims, occurred in the third decade after Halley's Comet.

That Taino sage was also the author of a story that appears in the original diary of the Admiral. In that story, he tells that when he was younger, he entered the cave of the Haitises to discover the origin of his race because that cave was known by his ancestors as the navel of the earth.

According to this legend, the origin of all his ancestors, including all the other indigenous groups of the far north and those of the far south, could be traced to that cave. He also relates that during his visit to the cave, he fell asleep for a long time. His son was still nursing at his mother's breast when he entered the cave; after his long sleep, when he returned to the tribe, the son was a young man.

When the other members of the tribe saw him, they were very surprised, as they thought he was one of their gods; he came out with a black and white beard that reached his feet and his hair reaching his calf. They could hardly understand him when he spoke, and immediately, they started bringing tributes to him because they thought he was really a god. He had to spend a great deal of time explaining to them the details of things and situations he remembered when he lived among them so that they would recognize him.

The account also describes certain visions he had while sleeping in the cave. In one of these visions, he recalls that he spent months or years walking through the cave, and when he reached one of the openings of the cave, he came to the surface and saw large tracts of land with lush nature and some strange animals, and then he returned to the cave and continued his journey to come out, which he did after another long time, through another opening. Coming to the surface, he sometimes saw more limited tracts of land that looked like islands surrounded by water on all sides. In other of his exits by the distant lands of the north and the distant lands of the south, he came across certain groups of people like those of his race, but fearful of them, he returned to his cave.

In another of these visions, he recalls that a group of white men arrived in a giant *Yola* very different from the ones they built; he says that when these men settled on land, they ate all the gold they found on their way, and they were lovers of war. After a long time, the white men brought other giant boats full of black men; these men were more peaceful, but they ate all the black coal on the land as well as some plants with sweet stems that resembled bamboo, and they amused themselves collecting rocks to build big houses for the white men.

Chapter 8

The centaurs

Many people thought that centaurs were a thing of the past. But once, in a place in the Caribbean known as The Dolorosa Village, a beast from the president's estate gave birth to two exceptionally beautiful centaurs, which soon became the talk of the whole country. The president was an authoritarian leader whom everyone feared, and as a result, many residents of the community devised numerous ways to please the president to ingratiate themselves with him and always have him on their side.

To please the president and be allowed to go to his estate, everyone began to praise the strange creatures. Many began to devise ways to celebrate the existence of the centaurs; thus, contests were held among the participants, and the child who best painted the image of the centaurs was awarded a prize and public recognition. From that moment on, classrooms in schools were flooded with the multicolored display of images of the centaurs. These precious images of the centaurs began to appear in all public offices and government institutions, as well as private institutions all over the country. It was also interesting to see that in all the national printing presses, when publishing their own books, the writers dedicated the first page to showing the image of the centaurs, just as they had previously done with the centaurs beloved mother, the beast. These images were always accompanied by a very expressive description or some poetic thought, as they used to do with their mother.

Also, photographs, drawings, and paintings of the centaurs appeared in all the textbooks for children and in the literacy campaigns that were carried out at the national level. The different poets and writers managed to wrap these images in a variety of plots and poems, narratives, and dramatic compositions so as not to tire the reader. Also, there were festivals, literary contests, book fairs, etc., in which the different writers exhibited their designs and diverse creative materials alluding to the presidential family.

From an early age, these two sons of the president began to receive an intensive education at home with highly specialized teachers in all branches of human knowledge. As a result, their influence would soon be felt throughout the country. On many occasions, they were seen at public ceremonial events in the company of their parents.

In the course of time, there were cases in which they were allowed to appear alone in press conferences, in which acts they began to show their unusual capacities and talents, flooding once again all the radio and written press and the national and international television stations. Above all, they were already performing specific public functions which were assigned to them by their parents.

When the centaurs became adults, their image before the public began to change; their master, the president, had become a dictator, and people began to despise him. Not only that, but their master also began to use them as an instrument to mistreat his enemies and opponents. Because of this, they became evil beings that harmed society.

After a continuo wave of attacks by the centaurs, a curse fell upon the people of Villa Dolorosa. Among the anomalies that appeared in some of the communities of the country due to centaurs' evil deeds were children suffering from metabolism problems and some other diseases. Great was the anguish of one particular family that struggled to cure a son who had a metabolism problem that caused him to develop an animal's body part every time he ate the meat of any kind of animal. If he ate chicken skin, in some parts of his body, the skin became the same as a chicken's; if he ate liver, his belly became swollen; if he ate leg broth, his feet would swell. They consulted many doctors, but still, nothing changed.

Some neighbors claimed that the child was under enchantment. Everyone in the community began to counsel the child's parents.

Take him to the "Señorita," they were told. The Señorita was the healer of the community. She had earned her name because she never married and dedicated her whole life to helping other people in the community and doing good with the supernatural powers she possessed. So, the boy was taken to the healer of the Dolorosa community. The

Señorita advised him to stop eating meat for some time and to eat only vegetables. From that day on, the boy became a vegetarian and began to feel well. After being cured of that illness, the child lived a long, normal life, but after some time, he died. The only strange problem was that when the child died, he turned into a small tree. The parents then decided to plant it in the backyard of the house.

To this day, everyone in the community refers to him as "Johnny the tree". There are those who claim that they once heard voices coming from the tree. Those who do not know the history of the tree are quite surprised when they hear these claims.

(Note: for a more complete version of this story, see my novel, *The Incredible Wedding of a Dictator*).

Chapter 9

The enchanted cave

In a picturesque place in the center of the Caribbean, one hundred and fifty kilometers northeast of the city of Santo Domingo is the so-called Cave of the Haitises, popularly known as "the enchanted cave" because of the countless legends and stories woven about the cave. Over time, thousands of curious people visited this place, some attracted by the enchanting natural beauty of the landscape and others because of their curiosity to find out to what extent the different legends or events that have occurred in this place are real.

Some scientists affirm that many of these legends could have their explanation in magnetic waves or forces emanating from the geological depths of this cave, as it is located exactly near the western vertex of the Bermuda Triangle, one of the deepest parts of the earth, and because it coincides with the line marked by the passage of hurricanes and earthquakes.

The truth is, everyone who visits this place is amazed by the beauty of the bay, its leafy cays, the whiteness of the sand, the transparency of the water, and the beautiful birds that swarm around this place. The natural landscape is attractive at any time of the year, but the variety and quantity of birds are even greater if you visit this place during the winter because, at that time of the year, almost all the birds from the north of the American Continent return to this place to escape from the rigor of the winter.

One of the beliefs associated with the cave is that many of the birds, as well as some other animals and the *ciguapas* (ciguapas are mysterious beings with inverted feet that face backward) that inhabit the place, have been transformations of human beings that have passed through the place over time.

A lot of people who have visited the site have reported seeing how some of these birds and other strange animals have approached them as if irritated the moment they approach the cave. It seemed as though they wanted to warn them of something strange that might happen to them when they entered the cave. Many do not take these incidents seriously, as they believe that it could be some protective birds or animals trying to intimidate the visitors because they pass very close to where they have hidden their nests and dens.

It is believed that when the visit is made during the full moon nights of the year, the enchanting and almost magical effect of the cave can be better felt, especially at night. However, what is most recommended is a visit during a very clear and radiant day, which is typical in the Caribbean area. Many of the visitors who have ventured into some of the cave's strategic points have reported having felt certain strange phenomena, such as chills, bristling of the skin and hair, an unexpected sweat breakout, and strange smells. Others claim that, when closing their eyes for a moment, they have had some visions.

One of the most common visions reported by visitors is that they claim to have seen, in a certain part of the cave, a giant island populated by dinosaurs, which can be seen from a distance in their natural environment as if they were watching a movie.

Another legend about the cave is that, just as this island was the beginning of European civilization for the entire American Continent, it is believed that the origin of all the primitive inhabitants of the continent—the Tainos, the Caribs, the Siboneyes, the Mayas, the Aztecs, the Incas, the Chibchas, etc.—could be traced to this cave. For this reason, many call it the navel of the earth. Many of these beliefs about the enchantments of that cave also arose from the stories told by a wise Taino, as can be seen in an ancient manuscript that appeared hidden somewhere in the cave.

Chapter 10

Why some birds do not fly

It is said that when God was walking on the earth, He had to spend a long time in the desert. In that inhospitable place, there was nothing to eat. And, naturally, He got hungry, and from time to time, He had to eat something to survive. His human form seemed to limit His power. Fortunately, the birds were mysteriously attracted by His presence. Each one of them brought Him something to eat. The smaller birds would bring

Him some of the most delicious small fruits they could find in the distant forest. The stronger birds, on the other hand, would bring him larger fruits that were also very delicious, such as apples, mangoes, pears, and strawberries.

As they paraded in their arduous but joyful task of providing something to eat for their Creator, one of the large birds, a little careless and tired, inadvertently dropped something near the Lord as it was flying away in front of Him. The Lord simply looked at the bird, and it fell to the ground. The bird continued to live; however, it could not fly again. It was the ostrich, and it seemed as if the Lord wished that the offspring of those birds were not able to fly, and that misfortune was passed down to every other species of heavy bird descended from it.

Chapter 11

Why ants like honey so much

Many believe that at the beginning of creation, ants were insects with the same characteristics as bees and that they also produced some of the richest honey that all other species liked. It is also said that they were all able to fly to capture the nectar of the flowers from which they produced their rich honey. Their misfortune began one day when one of the worker ants was looking for something to eat in the middle of a haystack.

There were also many animals there, and in the middle of that place, in the far east, was a manger with a child in it. A young mother had laid the child there because she had no other safe place to put her baby. The ant had come to this manger in search of some crumb of bread that the child had dropped on the straw. With the movement of the child, the ant was frightened, thinking it to be some other insect about to make it its prey.

Quickly, the toe of the little baby's foot was bitten by the ant, and the child cried out. The mother ran to see why the child was crying; she checked the child and saw nothing around him, apart from an ant lurking around the edge of the manger. Suspecting that it was an ant bite, she said something against such insects. The problem was that the ant never suspected that the baby in the manger was not like any other baby in the world. It was none other than the child Cupid, the son of the goddess Venus when he first came into the world.

It is said that Cupid is the son of Venus, the goddess of love and beauty, and Mars, the god of war. According to this story, Cupid would have been born in Cyprus, where his mother had to hide him in the woods and let him be cared for by wild animals because the god, Jupiter, wanted to kill him.

It was on that occasion that the incident with the daring ant happened while the child was in the care of his mother and before he had been left in the care of the wild animals.

The fact is that since then, the ant never returned to produce its rich honey, but instead, it is condemned to always be in search of something sweet wherever it goes, spending its whole life working hard and wishing to return to its original nature someday.

Chapter 12

Why mules do not reproduce

Lisa was a very intelligent child; from a very young age, she showed her curiosity to know all the mysteries and secrets of nature. She had observed very well that all species of animals reproduced and had their own younglings. However, one day it occurred to her to uncover why mules could not have babies like all the other animals she had seen.

So, she asked her mother, but she did not give her a proper answer.

"I don't know, my daughter. I hadn't noticed that," her mother answered. But she was restless in her pursuit to find the answer. So, one day, while visiting her great-grandmother's house, she decided to ask her. As her great-grandmother had lived all her life in contact with nature, she knew that her great-grandmother would be able to give her a good explanation. So, standing in front of her, she asked her:

"Great grandmom, why don't mules reproduce?" Her great-grandmother smiled at her and immediately began to explain why. She told her that God walked the earth a long time ago; the first time, He came not as an all-powerful being, but as a child, just like when she was a baby. An evil king learned from some magicians that this child would become the King of the world, and so he began to kill all the children because he did not know which of those children would be the one who would become king and a threat to his reign. His worried parents then ran away to the desert to protect their baby. As they went through the desert, the mother was riding with her baby on a mule, not a donkey, as many believe.

As they were going along the rocky part of the desert, the mule was very tired, and at that moment, a snake passed in front of the mule. The animal was scared and stumbled over a rock, and the snake, standing upright, propelled on the lower part of its tail, causing the mother and her child to fall to the ground. Fortunately, the fall didn't cause a scratch to the mother or the baby, but naturally, she was frightened by the incident. So being a little angry with the animal, she wished the animal would never have a child again because of what it had done. "You will never have young of your own again," she told the animal. In the same way, she said to the snake, "From now on, you will slither on the ground." From that moment on, the mule never again had young of its own like all the other beasts of the field, and the snake began to slither on its belly on the ground, as they do today.

Lisa, now incredibly pleased, pondered over her great-grandmother's explanation.

Chapter 13

The child who became an angel

It all started when I awoke very early one Good Friday morning after a deep sleep. Well, I thought it was just that—a great dream; but it was not so because when I woke up, I began to feel the promontories of my wings behind each shoulder; I felt that they were beginning to grow. They did not bother me; on the contrary, they gave me a sense of peace, and my body began to feel lighter. To test myself, I leaped into the air, like the first man who went to the moon, but I was surprised to find that I could soar quite a bit higher.

For a moment, I was a little disturbed as I began to reflect on what people would think of me now that I was an angel. They would think that I was a chicken, a giant eagle, or a condor. Suddenly, I realized that these absurd ideas were put in my mind by Satan because since I was a child, he began to show me glimpses; it seems that he recognized that someday I would be a good angel and that I could block many of his powers. So, as soon as I recognized the source of those thoughts, I began to get rid of them.

Then I started to feel happy, joyful, almost euphoric, though I still began to cover my tender wings for the next three days so that no one, not even my own family, would notice what was happening to me. But I no longer felt guilty about anything. When the day of the Resurrection arrived, I felt jubilant; sometimes, it seemed to me that I could be transfigured.

On the third day, the wings had grown so large that I could no longer hide them. So, before my family and the other neighbors of the neighborhood woke up, I decided to test myself. I went out at dawn, and between light and dark, I began to get off the ground. In fractions of a second, I found myself among the clouds. High in the sky, they were already beginning to light up by the sun's flashes in their multiple colors. I began to play with them as if they were big white cushions; I turned on them, spun in circles, and let myself fall. I thought I could spend a great part of my life in that game, but then I remembered that I had to return to reality down on earth with my family and friends.

It was not difficult for me to explain to my family; I decided that it was best if they accepted my new reality. I told them that my wings had started to grow in the early morning of Good Friday, and I had kept them covered to avoid causing any panic. However, on Resurrection Day, I could no longer hide them as they had developed to their natural size. I then asked them to touch the feathers and move them and to touch the trunk of the wings behind my shoulders to see that everything was real. I tried to make them relax because I saw the look of surprise and astonishment on their faces. I also saw my sisters' hair stand up when they touched me. One of them even fell to the ground from the shock that my appearance had caused, almost rendering her unconscious. But I immediately raised her in my arms, and within seconds, she opened her eyes and began to laugh. Everyone then burst out laughing.

When the neighbors began to arrive because of my siblings uproar, I did not worry at all; I did the same with them. Seeing them with their mouths open, as if they were also in a kind of trance, I approached them and made them touch me so that they would not be afraid at all. They soon became accustomed to my being an angel, and some of them began to think about how they could profit from my ability to fly. The cleverest were the children, who immediately asked me to pass them some *chichiguas, papelotes,* or kites that had become entangled in the tips of the trees. I was happy when I heard my little brother's voice just saying, "Woo! Woo! Wao!" Others wanted me to pass them some of the mangoes that were on the tips of the high branches, which they couldn't reach, even if they tried to throw rocks at them.

As rumors of my case spread throughout the community, the news reached the community priest, who wasted no time in coming to witness it for himself.

The children were often seen running through the streets as they shouted:

"Run! Run! Go and see the boy who became an angel!"

The priest came and started asking me questions, which I began to explain. I told him that since I was a child, I had always felt a strong desire to do good to other people. I realized that every time I wanted to do some charitable work, Satan would always try to stop me from doing it; he would give me strange looks. It was then that I decided to study the Holy Scriptures to find a way to confront him.

I also explained to the priest that some of my favorite readings were from Psalm 91, Isaiah chapter 53, and the story of Christ's Resurrection in the last chapter of the Gospels. I told him that as soon as I started reading those biblical portions, I never saw glimpses of the Evil One again. It was exactly what I was doing the night of Holy Thursday; I almost stayed up reading those biblical portions until I fell asleep and fell into a deep sleep. I began to dream that I could fly by waving my arms; I soared over the mountains, valleys, rivers, and sea, and then I felt joyful when I passed over the roofs of the houses and glided among the trees.

So, I spent the rest of the morning dreaming until I woke up on Good Friday, very early in the morning, and I started to feel the promontories of the wings coming out behind my shoulders. I tried to cover them with my jacket so as not to alarm my family, but when the third day came, which was the

Resurrection Day, I could no longer cover them. Then, when I went out to the yard to see if I could fly, I accidentally woke my family up, and I explained to them what had happened to me. The parish priest was so astonished and excited that, as he heard my story, even without meaning to, he uttered some religious words as if he were praying.

Anyway, everything was fine with him, and after he left, I thought that the only thing I didn't like about him was that he often wanted me to be in the church, just so the place would be filled with people. Sometimes, I also felt as if he was using me, just like the other neighbors who would always come to ask me to untangle some cable or wire that had gotten tangled above their houses.

After some time, I began to think about what my goal and function would be from now on as an angel. But I soon realized that God had sent me into this world for some purpose; that my life would be meaningless if I were to be limited to being just a simple henpecker, a harrier, or any fallen angel; that I would only produce distorted miracles, as in the case of one of those fallen angels. If that were the case, it would be all the same if I were to become a great beetle. But that is not my case; I believed that God had put me here with certain faculties beyond those of a human being for some purpose.

It was then that I understood that my purpose was to prepare the way for other angels of greater faculties than mine, who would come to this world when God so decided. So, to carry out my purpose, I began to incite and awaken the power of good in people so that they could overcome the evil impulses that Satan puts in the hearts and minds of men, as he wanted to do with me when I was a child. I also believed that what God had done with me, he would also do with other good people in this world because he would need many of us to help save his people. Therefore, our function is to prepare the way for the older angels who will come on special missions that have to do with the fulfillment of God's great plans.

Another faculty that God has given me is the ability to read the thoughts of others, even when I am not in their presence. This has helped me discover the diabolical plans of some individuals who were about to pour out their venom, and I blocked them. Also, I have noticed that when I am at church or on the street, and some of them want to say something against me, they remain quiet and flee when they notice my presence. This reaffirms those faculties that God has put in me.

On other occasions, I have felt that someone, somewhere, was about to perish, and I have rushed to their rescue. Once, someone was climbing a mountain, and one of his grip connections slipped. In another instance, a little girl fell into a pool at home due to her parents' carelessness. Similarly, a gas stove was about to explode in a house full of children in the absence of their parents. Additionally, an old man was about to be hit by a vehicle while crossing a downtown city street; in all these cases, I arrived on time to prevent it.

However, the experiences that I have enjoyed the most have been foreseeing and disarticulating macabre plans, which I was sure Satan had incited—such as terrorist plans and planned accidents, like altering the engine of a train or an airplane or sabotaging an industry. In short, I have had more fun disarticulating those satanic plans because I know that it was not only about endangering the life of a single individual but of hundreds, if not thousands, of people.

The level of my sanctity would not be limited to righting wrongs like St. Manuel or Don Quixote. In the case of St. Manuel, he taught a community to live blindly following a tradition, creating spiritual doubts in some of his close friends. In my case, I would incite people to follow the purpose of their lives that God had planted in their hearts, and I would awaken them and reactivate the seed of good that God has sown in them. I also would remind them of the way of St. Francis, the way of Mother Teresa, or the way of the Great Master of Galilee.

In the case of Don Quixote, instead of freeing a group of thugs who were on their way to prison by order of the King and who paid him by stoning him, I think it would be better to go to the prisons and make the penitential and judicial authorities see who were there by mistake and unjustly, after the plans and traps of ill-intentioned people that Satan had put in their paths.

This method has worked well for me even with people of other religions, whom I have awakened and reactivated only the seed of truth that God had placed in them to reconcile them. While to some, I said, "Remember that it is not about millions of gods, that there is only one true God." To others, I said, "Do not forget the teachings of your prophet, who told you that 'virtue is in being sincere worshippers of God... do good to others... your true enemy is Satan.' So that 'God knows all that you do.' If you keep these commandments, you, too, will hear the trumpet on Judgment Day for your eternal good."

Similarly, my worst struggle was with people involved in a world of nightmares, absurd governmental ordinances, and institutions of ill-intentioned men. To some, I spoke in dreams, and to others, I passed on the message God was sending them.

Among my greatest distractions or entertainment, I used to make use of the healing power of music, which I used as an excuse to practice the trumpet, which we will have to use someday for greater purposes. Well, many came to hear me play because they found relief, both for their physical ailments as well as for their mental and emotional problems.

Another thing I have discovered is that when I must rescue someone from fire, it does not affect me at all; I can go through a flame of fire in the same way I can go through a cloud or fog. God has given us the power to lead and even to go to war on His behalf. The only function I do not like is to destroy; I leave that to the older angels who will come after me.

Sometimes I am absent when it is time for praise up there, but when I return, I come back with more energy and strength of will to pursue my purpose and my good works with joy. So, God has made me something superior to men, but I do not boast of that because I do not act of my own accord.

At other times, we have special functions, such as when we served the Master of Galilee when he was tempted, and we also serve any person that He indicates to us. All this gives me joy because what we do here is only a rehearsal for what we will do when we are commanded on that day to blow the trumpet to serve the King of Kings and Lord of Lords. So, when God assigns us a mission, we all joyfully try to do our best because he has promised us that, among his legions of angels, only seven will have the special function when that great day arrives. That is why, among all of us, there always shines the hope of becoming one of the seven.

And, finally, another piece of advice I give you is this: do not forget that the woman was chosen to carry the greatest message of mankind, the Resurrection of Christ! So, listen to your fellow women because some of them will be the first to perceive the signs that the trumpets are approaching. Also, I have already warned my family that I will continue to do my mission until I am called from the earth. That they no longer must worry about my age or about my burial; that on the day of my call, I will simply be absent, and no one else will see me again until the Great Day of Trumpets!

The end.

Chapter 14

Hernan and Graciela - poverty

Somewhere in a large forest lived a poor woodcutter and his wife and two children, Hernan and Graciela. Even in good times, the family did not have enough to eat. At this time, the whole country was suffering from a terrible famine, and very often, the father could not even earn enough for a daily ration of bread for each of them. Amid this hardship, his wife died of an incurable disease, so he married another woman to help him raise his children. Unfortunately, the woman turned out to be very hard-hearted.

The father, however, made a great effort to manage to grow produce for food, and that sustained them for a long period of time. Hernan also contributed by finding food for the livestock and by selling fruits and vegetables like mangoes, eggplants, tomatoes, and other products from the vegetable garden in their backyard. Their hard work helped them to contain misery and famine for a long period of time.

But, inevitably, after some time came the lean cow season, which came at a time when even nature refused to be kind. A great drought set in that forced them to follow the stepmother's food rationing plan.

One night, when the poor man was thinking about the worry he felt because of his extreme poverty, he turned to his wife and said:

"What will become of us? How can we feed our children if we can't even feed ourselves?"

"I'll tell you what we could do," she said. "You'll see. First thing tomorrow morning, we'll take them deep into the forest, get them well settled with a fire to keep out the cold and a little bread to eat and leave them to their fate. As they will not find their way home, we will get rid of them."

"No, no, no," said the father. "I will do nothing of the kind. Do you expect me to abandon our children in the forest? Never! The vermin would attack them and tear them to pieces."

"If we don't get rid of them, the four of us will starve to death. You can start preparing the planks to build all our coffins."

She insisted again and again, without leaving him alone until the man gave in.

"Anyway, I don't like this idea at all," he said. I still feel very sorry for them..."

In the next room, the children were still awake. Their hunger was so intense that they could not fall asleep, and they heard every word their stepmother uttered.

Graciela was crying bitterly and said in a very low voice:

"Oh, Hernan, this will be the end of us!"

"Shut up," said Hernan. "I've come up with an idea; stop worrying."

As soon as the parents fell asleep, Hernan got out of bed, put on his old jacket, opened the bottom of the door, and crawled out. The moon was shining brightly, and the white pebbles in front of the house glittered like silver coins. Hernan squatted down and picked up as many pebbles as he could fit in his pockets.

Then he went back inside, got into bed, and whispered:

"Don't worry, Graciela. Go to sleep. God will take care of us. Besides, I have a plan."

At dawn, before the sun began to rise, the woman approached the children and removed their blankets.

"Come on! On your feet, you slackers! she shouted, "We'll go out into the woods to get firewood."

She handed them each a piece of dry bread and said:

"This is what you have for lunch, so don't eat it in a hurry, or you won't have anything else."

Graciela put the two pieces of bread in the pocket of her apron, as Hernan's pockets were full of stones, and immediately, they set off into the forest. From time to time, Hernan would stop and look back to see if he could still see the house until his father said to him:

"Hey, kid, what are you doing? Walk. Use your legs."

"I was looking at my white kitten. He's climbed up on the roof and is sitting there," said Hernan. He's saying goodbye to me".

"This boy is a fool," said the woman. That's not your kitten. It is the reflection of a sunbeam in the chimney."

Hernan had dedicated himself to throwing pebbles as he passed, one by one, and he looked behind him because he wanted to make sure that they left a visible trail.

Once they reached the heart of the forest, their father told them:

"Take a few branches. I'll light a fire so you don't freeze."

The children took some branches, made a big pile of them, and their father lit the fire. As the fire burned with a good flame, the woman said:

"Make yourselves comfortable, little ones. Lie down by the fire and take advantage of the warmth to sleep for a while. In the meantime, we'll go and cut some logs, and we'll come and get you when we've finished."

Hernan and Graciela stretched out by the fire. When they calculated that it was time for lunch, they ate their pieces of bread. They could hear the sounds of an axe not far from there and deduced that their father was working nearby. However, in reality, what they heard was not axes but the noise made by a branch that the father had tied to a trunk, causing it to swing with the wind and produce the banging noise they had mistaken for the sound of axes. The two children sat there for a long time, and little by little, they noticed their eyelids getting heavy and closing. As the sun began to set and it was getting darker, they lay close to each other and fell asleep.

When they woke up, night reigned around them. Graciela began to cry.

"We'll never find our way out!" said the girl as she sobbed."

"Wait until the moon rises," said Hernan, "and you will see what the plan is I told you about."

When the moon finally came out, it was very large and shining brightly, and the white stones Hernan had been throwing glittered like newly minted coins. Holding hands, the children followed the trail all night long, and just as dawn broke, they arrived at their father's house. The door was locked, and they knocked loudly. When the woman came out to open the door, her eyes opened wide, reflecting her displeasure.

“What a pair of wretches! You don't know how much we've worried about you!” And she hugged them so tightly that they could hardly breathe. “Why did you sleep so long? We thought you didn't want to come back!” And she pinched their cheeks as if she were truly happy to see them there again. A moment later, when their father came out and showed real joy on his face, they knew that he had not wanted to leave them.

So that time, they were spared. But not long after that, food became scarce again, and there were many, many people who were hungry. One night the children heard the woman talk to their father and say to him:

“This is going from bad to worse. We only have one loaf of bread left, and when it's gone, we're all going to starve. We must get rid of the children, and this time we must make sure we really get rid of them. The other time they must have used some sort of trick, but if we take them to a place in the forest that is too remote, then they won't find their way out.”

“I don't like that idea," said the father. “In the forest, there are not only vermin but also goblins, witches, and God knows what else. Wouldn't it be better to share this last loaf with the children?”

"Don't be foolish," said the woman. "That's a foolish thing to say. Your problem is that you're too soft. Soft and foolish." And she continued to criticize and insult him, and he was unable to defend himself. When you've given in once, you'll give in forever. The children were awake, and they heard the conversation. When the grownups were asleep, Hernan got up and tried to go outside again, but the woman had locked the bolt and hidden the key. However, when Hernan returned to bed, he tried to comfort his sister, telling her:

"Don't worry, Graciela. Now, sleep. God will protect us."

The next day, at dawn, the woman woke them up, just as she had done the other time, and gave them each a piece of bread, although this time it was even smaller. And as they went deeper into the forest, Hernan crumbled the bread and dropped crumbs along the way, often stopping to check that they were visible.

"Walk, Hernan, don't stop," said his father, "and stop looking behind you all the time."

"I was trying to see if I could spot my pigeon on the roof of the house," said Hernan. He went up there to say goodbye to me."

"You fool," said the woman. "It's not your pigeon. It's the sun shining on the chimney. Come on, walk briskly."

Hernan did not look back but continued crumbling the bread in his pocket and dropping crumbs from time to time. The woman forced them to walk faster, and that day they went deeper into the forest to places they had never been before.

At last, when they'd gone too deep into the forest, the woman said:

"That's fine."

And again, they lit a fire to keep the children waiting.

"Don't you dare move from here," the woman told them. "Sit down and don't move until we come back. We have enough to worry about. All we must do now is look for you. We'll be back by sundown."

The children sat there until it seemed like noon, and then they shared the piece of bread that had been left for Graciela because Hernan did not have a single crumb of his left. After eating, they fell asleep, and the whole day went by, and nobody went to look for them.

When they awoke, it was already dark.

"Calm down, Graciela; don't cry," said Hernan. "When the moon rises, the crumbs of bread will be visible, and then we will find our way back home." The moon came out, and they began to look for the trail of crumbs but found none. The thousands of birds living in the forest and in the fields, as well as the ants, had eaten everything.

"You'll see how we find our way," said Hernan.

But, after trying many directions, they found it impossible to find their way home. They spent all night walking and then walked all day, but to no avail. They were lost. And moreover, they were hungry, terribly hungry, as the only thing they had eaten all day was a handful of berries they found in the forest. Eventually, they felt so tired that they lay down at the foot of a tree and fell asleep right there.

On the third day, they woke up again and tried with great effort to get to their feet. They were still lost and had the feeling that every step they took made them go deeper and deeper into the heart of the forest. If they did not find someone to help them soon, they would end up dying there.

But at noon, they saw a snow-white bird perched on a tree branch. It sang so beautifully that they stopped to listen to its trills. Then it spread its wings and soared up, landing on another tree a little farther away, and the two children followed. Once perched on the new branch, the bird began to sing again, and then it flew another distance. As it did not fly very fast, the children were able to follow its lead; it seemed as though it was guiding them. Then suddenly, they found themselves in front of a small house. The bird had landed, this time on the roof, which had a strange appearance.

"That ceiling is made of cake!" Hernan exclaimed.

As for the walls:

"They are made of bread!" said Graciela.

"And the windows are made of sugar."

The poor children were so hungry that it didn't even occur to them to call first and ask permission. Hernan broke a piece of the roof, and Graciela broke a window, and the two sat down and began to eat without any hesitation. After a few bites, they heard a soft voice coming from inside the house, saying:

"Eat, eat, little mouse, who eats my little roof?"

And the children answered:

"It is a gust of wind because the Child of

Heaven blows."

And after saying that, they continued eating, as their hunger was voracious. Hernan liked the taste of the roof so much that he took another piece, and Graciela also carefully tore off another piece of glass from the window and began to take one bite after another. Suddenly, the door opened, and an old woman appeared; she was so old that she limped a lot when she walked. Hernan and Graciela were so stunned that they stopped eating and stared at her with their mouths full.

The old woman shook her head and said to them:

"Don't be afraid, little ones! Who brought you to this place? Come on, little ones, come in and rest in this tasty place; you'll feel as safe as at home!"

She pinched them affectionately on the cheeks, took them each by the hand, and led them into the little house. And it was as if the old woman knew they were about to arrive, for they found inside a table set with two chairs, and she served them a delicious meal of milk and fritters sprinkled with sugar and spices, along with apples and nuts.

Then she showed them to a room where there were a couple of beds laid neatly with snow-white sheets. Hernan and Graciela fell asleep instantly. But the friendly manner of that old woman was only an appearance. She was an evil witch, and she had built that house to lure and trap children. Every time she caught one of them, whether it was a boy or a girl, she killed them, cooked them, and then ate them. Every time she caught a child, it was like the biggest party for her. Like all witches, her eyes were red, and her sight was not very far-reaching. But she had a very good sense of smell, and as soon as there was a human being in the vicinity, she knew about it. When she saw that Hernan and Graciela were snug in their beds, the witch cackled and rubbed her gnarled hands together, relishing the moment.

"I've got them!" she cackled, her voice high-pitched. "They can't get away now!"

The next morning, she got up and went to the children's room. She stood for a few moments, checking them out. They were still asleep. Those rosy cheeks of the children were so appetizing that she had to restrain herself from grabbing them at that very moment. "What tasty morsels," she thought.

Then, she took Hernan and, before the child could scream, dragged him out of the house and left him locked in a cage inside a shed. The child began to scream, but to no avail, for no one could hear him. Then the witch woke Graciela saying to her:

"Wake up, lazybones! Go fetch water from the well, and then you'll cook something for your brother. He's in the shed, and I want to fatten him up. And when he's fat enough, I'm going to eat him."

Graciela began to cry; she had no choice but to comply with all the witch's orders. And so it was that Hernan was served the most delicious delicacies every day while Graciela had to make do with sucking on crab shells.

With her limping gait and leaning on her cane, the witch went every morning to the shed and told Hernan:

"Hey, boy! Stick your finger out; let's see if you've put on enough weight."

But Hernan, who was very clever, pulled out a bone he had found on the floor through the bars, and the witch, with her red eyes, looked at it and thought it was the child's finger. And she couldn't understand why Hernan still hadn't put on weight.

A few weeks went by, and the witch still thought Hernan was too skinny. But thinking about how rosy his cheeks were, she could wait no longer and said to Graciela:

"Hey, girl! Go get some water. Bring lots of water. Fill the kettle to the top, and we'll boil the water. Fat or skinny or plump, I'm going to slaughter it tomorrow and boil it and make a good stew out of it."

Poor Graciela began to cry and cry, but she had no choice but to obey the witch's order and fetch water.

"My God, help us! If we had been eaten by wolves in the forest, at least we would have died together!"

"Stop whining," said the witch. "It won't do you any good."

The next day, Graciela lit the fire in a cavity under the oven.

"We'll bake the bread first," said the witch. "I've already kneaded the flour. Let's see that fire; is it alive enough?"

She dragged Graciela to the door of the oven, and under the base, which was an iron grate, the fire was burning brightly, spitting sparks and very red flames.

"Get in there and see if the fire burns well," said the witch. "Go on, don't dawdle. In you go!"

Of course, what the witch wanted to do was lock her in the oven as soon as Graciela looked out so that she could cook her too. But the little girl guessed the witch's intentions and said:

"I don't quite understand. Do I have to look out there? How do I do it? I don't know how."

"You'll be foolish," said the witch. "Get out of the way. I'll teach you. It's easy as pie."

The witch ducked her head and put it in the oven. And as soon as she did, Graciela gave her such a push that the witch lost her balance and fell inside. Graciela immediately closed the door and secured it with an iron bar. From inside the oven came all kinds of dreadful screams, terrible shrieks, and moans, but Graciela covered her ears and ran outside. The witch burned to death in the oven.

Graciela ran to the shed and screamed:

"We are saved, Hernan! That old witch is dead!"

Hernan jumped out, as happy as a bird when its cage is opened. How happy the two children were! They hugged each other, jumped for joy, and kissed each other on the cheeks. They had nothing more to fear, so they entered the house and began to look everywhere. In every corner, they found trunks and drawers full of precious stones.

"They are better than pebbles!" said Hernan, putting a few beautiful stones in his pockets.

"I'm going to take some too," said Graciela, as she stuffed a bunch of them in her apron pockets.

"And now we can leave this place," said Hernan. "Let's get away from these witch-infested forests."

They started walking, and after a few hours, they reached the shore of a lake.

"We won't be able to cross it," said Hernan. "I don't see any bridge."

"There's no boat either," said Graciela. "Look over there, a big, strong swan, a white swan! I'm going to see if he can help us cross."

And she yelled at him:

"Hey, swan, you are handsome, strong swan!

Could you give us a bit of luck? Help us get

to the other side of these deep, cold waters."

The swan swam towards them, and Hernan rode on top of it.

"Come on, Graciela, you come up too!" he spoke.

"No! That would be too much weight!" Graciela said, "You'd better take us one at a time."

And so, the good swan did, first taking one child to the other side of the lake and then the other. When they were safe and sound on the other shore, they continued walking and, little by little began to recognize the forest they were in. Finally, they distinguished their house in the distance and ran towards it. And they threw themselves into their father's arms. The poor man had not had a moment of peace since he had left his children in the forest. Shortly after that sad day, his wife died, and he was left all alone and poorer than ever. But Graciela showed him the jewels she kept in the pockets of her apron, and Hernan also threw on the table the handfuls of precious stones he had taken.

So, all their sorrows ended at that moment, and they lived happily for the rest of their days.

Colorín colorado, this story is over.

Chapter 15

The elves

Once upon a time, there was a shoemaker who, through no fault of his own, became poorer and poorer, so much that he had hardly enough leather left to make a single pair of shoes. He cut the leather in the afternoon with the idea of sewing the shoes the next morning and then went to bed. He was very clear about his plans, so he said his prayers and then slept peacefully.

He woke up the next morning, ate a piece of dry bread, and sat down at his workbench. To his surprise, he saw that the shoes had been made. He was dazzled. He picked them up and looked at them from every possible angle. Every stitch was done to perfection; every part of the shoe was in place. He would not have been able to do any better.

Soon after, a buyer came in who needed shoes in exactly that size, and he liked that pair so much that he bought them, paying a good price for the shoes.

With that money, the shoemaker could buy enough leather to make two more pairs of shoes, and so he did. And, in the same way as the other time, he cut the leather in the afternoon with the intention of continuing the work the next morning, this time in very good spirits. But he had no need to continue when he awoke, as the shoes had already been made, just as the previous day, as if they had been sewn by a master of the trade.

He soon found buyers for the two pairs, which made him enough profit to buy leather to make four new pairs. He bought the leather, cut them, and the next morning the shoes had all been made. He then sold them, and this continued for a while. Every evening, he would cut the leather, and the next day the shoes would appear made. In this way, he soon found himself making good fortune, and it was not long before he became a rich man.

One evening, as Christmas was approaching, he cut the leather as usual to make more shoes, and, as he was about to go to bed, he said to his wife:

"What do you say if we stay up tonight and see if we can find out who has been helping us?"

His wife thought it was a good idea, so they lit a lamp and stood waiting behind a coat rack in the corner of the workshop, hiding behind the coats.

At midnight, two little naked men slipped under the door, jumped up onto the workbench, and immediately set to work, sewing all the shoes at a speed that seemed incredible to the shoemaker. They did not stop until they had finished the whole task, then left the shoes on the bench and left through the door again.

The next morning, the shoemaker's wife said:

"It seems to me that we should return the favor to these little men. After all, they've made us rich, and you see them as poor things, walking around without proper clothing to protect them from the cold. I'm going to sew them some shirts and some jackets, some underwear and pants, and I'll also knit them two pairs of socks. And you could make them some slippers."

"That's a good idea," said the shoemaker, and they both set to work.

That evening, they left all the clothes on the bench in place of the leather to make more shoes and went back to hide to see what the little men were doing. The two of them came in at midnight, jumped onto the bench as they had done the other time, ready to get to work, but stood there in surprise at the sight of all those clothes and began to scratch their heads in bewilderment. At last, they understood what it was all for, jumped for joy, and got dressed at once. Dressed up as well as they could, they ended up singing:

We have never been better off in our lives.

But in the future,

we will only be assistants for the occasion!

They jumped off the bench, nimble as kittens, and kept jumping and hopping over the chairs, the bench, the hearth, and the windowsill, and then they slipped under the door and disappeared. Well, upon seeing all the items, they concluded that the cobbler no longer needed their help and decided to return on occasion at Christmas and other times when they had plenty of work to do.

So, the shoemaker continued to do his work for all the inhabitants of the community. He continued to make his shoes, only now, he made them much better, thanks to the techniques he had learned from those clever little elves; for, in addition to the shoes of the common customers, there was never a lack of those for the student, the mayor, the schoolteacher, and the doctor.

The shoemaker continued to make progress. From then on, business was always good, and he and his wife lived happily for the rest of their lives.

Chapter 16

Snow White

On a winter's day, when the snowflakes were falling like feathers, a queen sat at her window, which had a frame of the blackest mahogany imaginable. She opened the window to look up at the sky, and as she moved her hand, she pricked herself, and three drops of blood fell on the snow that covered the sill. Seeing how beautiful the combination of red and white was, she said to herself, "I would like to have a child as white as snow, as red as blood, and as black as this window frame."

And soon after, she had a little daughter who was as white as snow and as red as blood, and as black as mahogany, and they called her Snow White. The queen died as soon as her child was born.

A year later, the king married another woman. She was beautiful but also proud and arrogant, and she could not stand the idea that there was another woman who was more beautiful than her. She had a magic mirror, and every morning she would stand in front of it, look at her reflection, and say:

Mirror, magic mirror, which is the fairest in the kingdom?

To which the mirror would respond:

Your Majesty, you are the most beautiful of all women.

And she was very pleased to hear it, for she knew that the mirror could only tell the truth.

Meanwhile, Snow White was growing up and was becoming more beautiful. At the age of seven, she was as pretty as a spring day, and in fact, she was prettier than the queen.

So, one day, when the queen asked her mirror:

Tell me, magic mirror, which is the most beautiful in the kingdom?

This time, the mirror responded:

You are still beautiful, your majesty, but Snow White is now much more so.

The queen was terrified when she heard this. Envy began to churn in her guts, and her complexion, until then perfect, took on a yellowish-green color. From then on, every time she looked at Snow White, she felt her heart harden because she was filled with malevolent hatred. Envy and pride grew inside the queen like weeds, and she found no peace, day or night. Not being able to bear it any longer, she called one of the king's hunters and told him:

"Take that girl to the deepest part of the forest. I never want to see her again in my life. Before you return, make sure she is dead, and bring her lungs and liver with you as proof."

The hunter did as he was told and took Snow White into the deepest part of the forest, and then he took out the bush knife. But when he was about to plunge it into the innocent girl's heart, she began to beg:

"Spare my life, I beg you, hunter. I promise I will flee into the heart of the forest and never return home!"

Because she was so pretty, the hunter took pity on her and said:

"Poor child. Go away from here; run far away."

"The wild beasts of the forest will eat her soon enough anyway," he thought to himself, but knowing that he wouldn't have to kill her himself, his heart felt as if a heavy burden had been lifted from him.

Out of nowhere, a young wild boar emerged from the bushes, and the hunter killed it, tore out its lungs and liver, and took them back to present them to the queen as proof of Snow White's death. The wicked queen ordered the cook to salt and pepper the offal, dredge it in flour, and fry it. She ate it without leaving a scrap. And that was, the queen thought, the end of Snow White.

Snow White, however, had been left alone in the forest and did not know at first what to do. She looked around, but nothing she saw in the leaves and bushes gave her the slightest indication that anyone was nearby. So, she felt very afraid and ran away, ignoring the sharp stones and the thorny brambles, and the animals that jumped in her path. And she ran and ran, and just as daylight was fading and the night was approaching, she saw a little house. She knocked at the door, but no one was there, so she went in and tried to rest.

In that little house, everything was very small, but she found it all very neat and tidy. By the fire, there was a pot of stew, and she saw a table set with a tablecloth as white as snow, and on it seven little bowls, with a slice of bread beside each one, and seven knives and seven forks and spoons, and the same number of little cups. Upstairs, she found seven little beds, all in a row. They were nicely made up, with snow-white sheets, and next to each bed was a bedside table with a little glass and toothbrush.

Snow White was hungry and thirsty, so she ate some of the stew that was hot in the pot, took a little piece of each slice of bread, and drank a sip of wine from each little cup. Then, realizing that she was exhausted, she went to lie down on one of the little beds upstairs, but it was too small for her. Then she tried another and finally found one that fit her. So, she said her prayers, lay down, closed her eyes, and fell asleep in a flash.

After a long time, when night had fallen, the owners of the little house arrived. They were seven little dwarfs who made their living by working at the mine, extracting gold from the depths of the mountains. They went in and lit their miner's lamps. And, at once, they noticed that things were not as they had left them.

"Someone has sat in my chair!"

"Someone has eaten from my bowl!"

"Hey, look, someone took a bite of my bread!"

"Someone has used the ladle and helped himself to some stew!"

"And they used my knife!"

"And they used my fork!"

"And they drank from my cup!"

They gawked at each other. They all looked up at the ceiling together, tiptoed up the stairs, looked at their beds, and whispered:

"Someone has tried my bed!"

"And mine...!"

"And mine...!"

“And mine...!”

“And mine...!”

“And mine...!”

“Hey, look what's here!”

The seventh dwarf had found Snow White asleep in his bed. They all tiptoed over to her and gazed at her with rapt attention. The light from one of the lamps illuminated the beautiful face resting on the white pillow.

“What a beautiful creature!”

“Who can it be?”

“Don't wake her up! She sleeps soundly...”

“What a pretty face!”

“Where did it come from?”

“It is a mystery, brothers! An unfathomable mystery...!”

“Let's go back downstairs. We must figure out what to do.”

They tiptoed down again and sat around the table.

“Poor thing, she looks exhausted!”

“We'd better not wake her up.”

“Not even tomorrow at dawn; it would be too early for her.”

“She may have fled from a witch who was chasing her.”

“What a fool you are! There's no such thing as witches!”

“She looks like an angel to me.”

“Yes, suppose it is. But where am I going to sleep? She's sleeping in my bed.”

The other six agreed to share their beds with him and that it would be best if he slept for an hour in each of the others' beds. And they all went to sleep.

The next morning, when Snow White awoke to find the seven dwarfs staring at her (for they had been awake and dressed for quite some time), she was alarmed.

“Don't be scared, damsel!”

“We are friends!”

“Even if we are not very handsome...”

“We won't do you any harm.”

“We promise you!”

“You will be safe here.”

"Tell us, what is your name?"

"They call me Snow White," she said.

They asked her where she had come from, how she had found her way to their cottage, and many other things, and she told them that her stepmother had tried to kill her, that the hunter had spared her life, and that she then, in a panic, had started running through bushes and brambles until she came across the cottage.

The dwarfs retreated to a corner of the room and began to talk among themselves in a very low voice, and then returned to her side and said:

"You are in charge of cleaning the house."

"From sweeping and mopping, you know, all that."

"And cooking! Don't forget to cook!"

"Yes, cooking and making the beds."

"And to do the laundry."

"And sewing and knitting and mending the socks."

"Then you can stay with us and use everything in this house."

"I will, and I will put all my heart and goodwill into it!" said Snow White.

And so it was that they came to settle this agreement, and from then on, Snow White oversaw running the house. In the mornings, all the dwarfs would go walking to the mountain in search of gold and copper and silver, and when they returned at nightfall, they would find supper ready and the little house clean and tidy.

In the daytime, naturally, Snow White was left alone, and the dwarfs warned her:

"Go carefully because if your stepmother found out you were still alive, she would try to track you down. Don't open the door for anyone!"

At the palace, the queen had eaten the liver and lungs that she thought were Snow White's. Not long after, the fear that caused her to look into the magic mirror was rekindled. So, she decided to look into it. She asked the mirror:

> *Tell me mirror, magic mirror, which is the most beautiful in the whole kingdom?*

And she got the most frightful shock when the mirror responded:

> *Majesty, you are very beautiful, but far away from here, in the deepest forest, with the seven dwarfs, Snow White lives now, and she is the most beautiful in the world.*

The queen recoiled in horror, for she knew very well that the mirror never lied, and she understood that the huntsman had deceived her. Snow White was still alive! All her thoughts turned to a single question: how could she now kill Snow White? If she, who was the queen, was not the most beautiful in the whole world, envy would torment her day and night.

The queen proceeded with her malevolent plan to kill Snow White. She used a lot of makeup until she became unrecognizable, taking on the appearance of an old huckster. She went to the house of the seven dwarfs and knocked on the door. At that hour, they were far away, working in the depths of the mine.

Snow White, who was making the beds, heard a knock and opened an upstairs window.

"Good morning," she said. "What are you selling?"

"Beautiful lace and precious ribbons," said the queen, looking up. "Do you want to see my wares, girl? Look at this one, how pretty!"

And she showed her a lace of silk thread. Snow White saw that it was indeed beautiful and thought that the old woman had an honest expression. She was in no danger if she let her in.

She ran downstairs, unfastened the locks, and stared raptly at a lace bodice.

"Do you want to try it on?" asked the woman, who looked like a genuine huckster. "My goodness, you creature. You really need someone to take care of you. Come, little one, I'll tighten your bra with this pretty ribbon."

Without the slightest suspicion, Snow White allowed the old woman to pass all the ribbon through each of the bodice's eyelets. Then the old woman began to squeeze tighter and tighter, and finally, the bodice was so tight around her chest that she couldn't even breathe. Snow White's eyes blinked rapidly, her lips quivered, and she suddenly collapsed to the floor.

"You are not so beautiful now that you are dead," murmured the old woman, who walked quickly away.

The dwarfs arrived not long after, as it was getting dark. When they saw Snow White unconscious on the floor, they were terrified. They checked her and soon discovered what was wrong with her and quickly cut the ribbon so that she could breathe again. Little by little, she came to her senses and was able to tell them what had happened.

"I'm sure you know who that peddler was, don't you?"

"Was the evil queen!"

"It could only be her."

"Be careful, Snow White. Be very, very careful!"

"Remember, you must always be on guard."

"Don't let anyone in, absolutely no one!"

Meanwhile, the queen was running back to the palace. As soon as she was locked in her room, she looked at herself in the mirror and asked:

Tell me mirror, magic mirror, which is the most beautiful in the whole kingdom?

And the mirror responded:

Your Majesty, you are very beautiful,

but the dwarfs cut the ribbon,

and brought Snow White back to life.

She's still the most beautiful in the world.

Hearing this, the queen felt a terrible pressure grip her heart, and the blood was so tight in her veins that she thought even her eyes were about to burst.

"Is she still alive? She's still alive! We'll see what happens to her now! I swear she won't be alive for long."

The queen knew the art of witchcraft. She crushed some leaves of strange herbs in the mortar, pronounced a spell, and then dipped a comb in the juice she extracted from those herbs. She had created a deadly poison. With the help of another bit of magic, she changed her appearance completely so that she looked nothing like the old woman from the other time and set out on her way to the dwarves' house.

Meanwhile, the dwarfs, who were sure that the wicked queen would return, prepared a plan to protect Snow White because they suspected that the evil old woman would come back for her. They looked for two brave dogs to guard the house and wait for the evil queen.

Arriving at the dwarfs' house on this second visit, she knocked on the door and said in a loud voice:

"I sell all kinds of trinkets! I bring combs and pins and mirrors! Ornaments for the prettiest girls!"

Snow White looked out of an upstairs window and said:

"I can't let you pass. I'm not allowed to. You better leave."

"It's all right with me, little one. I won't even cross the threshold," said the old woman, "but I'm sure no one will mind if you take a look at what I've got. Look, isn't this comb lovely?"

And indeed, it was a beautiful comb. Snow White thought that by taking a look at the old woman's wares, nothing could happen to her. She made a firm decision not to receive the evil queen, but not being sure that it was her, and feeling protected by the dogs of the dwarfs, she succumbed to the temptation to see the goods brought by the supposed seller when the latter tried to deceive her again. So, the evil queen tried to deceive her a second time. When she was about to enter the dwarfs' house where Snow White was, the dogs remained silent, waiting for her to approach the place.

Snow White ran downstairs, unfastened the bolts, and stood spellbound, looking at a beautiful comb. The guard dogs of the dwarfs, who had already sensed the evil queen's malignant sense of smell, took advantage of the moment when Snow White opened the door, and without barking or even giving the evil queen a chance to open her mouth, they attacked her, biting her to pieces, and finished her off in an instant.

These dwarfs were very good-spirited individuals, but they felt that they should do something to protect and save Snow White from the wicked queen's mischief.

After a short time, the little dwarfs arrived home. When they arrived in front of the little house, they were horrified by what they saw: the inert, disfigured body of the evil queen, but at the same time, they were happy to see Snow White alive, who was able to tell them what had happened, and they immediately recognized that their plan of protection had worked.

The dwarfs decided to get rid of the queen's body, or what was left of it. They dug a hole in the middle of the forest and buried the evil queen with the determined help of Snow White. Once again, they warned her again that she had nothing to worry about if she did not lose her head and did exactly what they told her to do. That is, never to open the door to anyone at all.

At the palace, the king, who was not only suspicious of his wife but was convinced of her wickedness and the hatred she had developed against Snow White, also devised a plan to find his daughter and rescue her. He then called the most skilled people of his kingdom to accompany him and help him with his goal, and hoping to find his daughter alive, he went to the heart of the forest to look for her.

After a long walk at dawn, they finally came across the dwarfs' cottage just before they left to go to work in the mine. When the father realized that his daughter was alive and well under the care of the dwarfs, he was overjoyed. He immediately identified himself to the dwarfs and asked them to let him see his daughter to make sure she was alright. They had a brief consultation on the side and then agreed to let the father meet his daughter, pointing out that she was still upstairs sleeping.

As the king made his way upstairs, the little girl had already been awakened by the noise of the footsteps coming up the stairs in the direction of her room. It is difficult to describe the intense emotion and joy the father felt seeing his daughter safe and sound and under no spell, as he had assumed. With his eyes filled with tears of emotion, he hugged and kissed her, explaining to her how much he had suffered and the pain he felt from her absence and suffering, being away from her home.

He immediately went downstairs to the dwarfs with his daughter and expressed his gratitude that his daughter was doing so well in the care of such sweet and generous souls. The father told them that he would take his daughter with him and that, to compensate them for the good treatment they had given her, he would let them work in the mines in his territories and also help them to build a bigger house, as they deserved it for the good treatment they had given his daughter.

As usual, the dwarfs held a brief consultation to themselves, then indicated that they accepted his offer and placed themselves at his disposal. Snow White, too, thanked them for their good treatment and for the care they had taken of her.

The dwarfs, after meeting, also told the father that they took pity on him for losing his daughter and that they were convinced he would know how to treat Snow White in the most suitable way and that they therefore gave him permission to take her with him to his kingdom.

Before leaving, the dwarfs explained to the father how they had saved the child from the queen's evil spell and what had happened to the evil queen when she was about to make her second attack on the child, and the plan they had devised to get the two guard dogs for the girl's protection and all that had happened. The father did not express any remorse or guilt for what had happened because he understood the importance of having saved his daughter and that the evil queen deserved everything that happened to her because of the diabolical plan she had conceived against his innocent daughter. After their greetings, they said goodbye and returned to their palace.

After a short while, the king complied with everything he had offered the dwarfs.

So, the third visit, then, was that of the father, who discovered Snow White safe and sound. He then took her to the palace, where, after some time, one summer morning, she had the chance to meet a prince who accidentally entered the king's territories while chasing his falcon and one of his hunting animals.

Now, let's see everything that happened in that encounter. After a while, when the girl had grown up, a prince was passing through the forest one radiant morning in the summer days, hunting. As he was following behind his falcon, which was chasing prey, he passed through Snow White's Garden. Upon seeing her, the prince fell madly in love with her; so elated was he by her exuberant beauty that he opened the door to what his heart felt and exclaimed:

> "O my lady, hope of my glory, rest and relief of my sorrow, joy of my heart! I thank heaven for setting before me the purest beauty on this radiant summer morning." To which Snow White replied:

"Lord, your much deserving, your extreme graces, and the sweetness of your words have caused me, for a moment, to be troubled before you, but echoing in my heart, I would beg you that I wish you would never depart from my presence."

"I love you more than anything else in the world. Come with me to my father's castle and accept my invitation to be my wife."

Snow White fell in love with him at once, and the wedding was immediately arranged with all the pomp and magnificence of the place. It was the most luxurious and famous wedding in living memory in the whole kingdom, and the two lived happily and contentedly all their long lives.

It is worth mentioning here that among those present at the great wedding feast were the seven dwarfs, who had been invited by the king in gratitude for the good treatment given to his daughter and to partake in the banquet prepared for all the guests of honor.

Chapter 17

Florinda and Joel

Once upon a time, in the middle of a thick forest, there was an old woman who lived alone in a very old castle. The old woman was a very powerful witch, so every day, she would transform herself into a cat or an owl. And at night, she would change back into her human form. She knew how to hunt birds and other prey; she would sacrifice them and roast them on the fire and then feed on them. If a man came to the vicinity of the castle and approached within a hundred paces of the castle walls, she would cast an evil spell on him, causing him to be completely paralyzed until she decided to set him free. However, if the one who came so close to the castle was a girl, the old woman would transform her into a bird and force her into a wicker basket. Then she would take the wicker basket and carry it up to a room in the castle where she kept more than seven thousand birds, each one in a different basket.

At that same time, there was a girl who lived on the outskirt of the village, called Florinda. People said she was the most beautiful in the whole kingdom. She was engaged to a handsome young man named Joel. It was not long before the wedding, and what they liked most was being together. One afternoon, they decided to go for a walk in the woods to be alone.

"But let's be careful and not get too close to the castle," Joel cautioned.

It was a beautiful afternoon. The sun rays were bouncing on the trunks of the trees, and the warm tones of the sunlight were producing a strong contrast with the dark green of the foliage. In the branches of the old birch trees, the turtledoves were cooing. Although she did not know why, Florinda began to cry. She sat down in a corner lit by the sun, let out a sigh, and Joel sighed too. They were as sad as if they were close to death. Such was the intensity of the emotions that overwhelmed them that they did not realize where they were and ended up lost in the forest, not knowing how to return to their village.

The sun had not yet fully set. Half of its circumference was below the hills, and the other half was still peeping over them when Joel, trying to find his way back, pushed aside the branches of a thicket and saw the castle walls rising a few paces from where they stood. He got such a shock at the sight of them that he almost fainted. And just at that moment, he heard Florinda singing:

Little bird, pretty little bird of the red

circle, you who sing this song so sad;

sweet little bird of the red circle, look at

the sweet turtledove that...

But she did not finish the song, and at that moment, Joel heard a nightingale singing. He was horrified to find that Florinda had disappeared, and in her place was a nightingale perched on a branch. What's more, an owl with very yellow eyes was flying around it. It circled over the nightingale three times, hooting incessantly:

"U-uuh! U-uuh! U-uuh!"

Joel was paralyzed, still as stone; he couldn't move or scream or blink. By then, it was almost dark. The owl flew away into some bushes, out of Joel's sight, but then the young man heard a rustling of leaves, and suddenly the owl changed into an old woman with yellowish, wrinkled skin, very red eyes, and a sharp, aquiline nose, the tip almost touching her chin. Muttering under her breath, she moved closer and picked up the nightingale that was still perched on the branch, and then took it with her.

Joel couldn't scream or move a muscle. And the nightingale and the old woman disappeared from his sight. Joel's greatest fear was that the witch might eat the bride, now turned into a bird, as she used to do with many other trapped birds she fed on.

After a short time, the old woman returned empty-handed. And in a hoarse, raspy voice, she said:

"Zachiel, when the moonlight illuminates the basket, set the boy free."

Joel noticed that all his limbs had regained their flexibility, and before long, he was able to move again. He then knelt in front of the old woman and exclaimed:

"Give me back my dear Florinda!"

"Never!" The witch replied, "She will never return to your side!"

The young man begged, screamed, and cried, but he knew right away that she was not going to change her mind. She didn't even stop to listen to his pleas and left him there, crying.

"What will become of me?" Joel sobbed.

He left the castle and walked to a village where no one knew him. There he was given a job as a shepherd, and he lived in that village for a long time. He often went back to the forest and stared at the castle but never came too close.

Meanwhile, it was remarkable the fear and shock that this witch had instilled in the inhabitants of all the communities that were at a certain distance around the castle due to the disappearances of the people who approached the place where the witch lived.

Due to the pain Joel felt at having lost his beloved, one day, he had a revelation in the middle of a dream. He dreamed that he had to find a white rose with a divine touch to find a solution to this evil. According to his revelation, finding a white rose with a divine touch was the only thing that could break the witch's spell.

After some time exploring the fields and gardens, he remembered that in the dream, he had been told that it had to be a flower with a divine touch. So, he dedicated himself to searching in the religious temples of the whole region until, one day, in the temple of his community, the candor and elegance of a white rose that adorned the image of the Child Jesus caught his attention. When he approached the rose and touched it, he instantly felt a divine fire in his heart, and at that very moment, he thought that it was the rose with a divine touch that he had seen in his revelation, with which he could break the spell of the witch of the castle. The dream was very strange, but its indications were very precise. He dreamed that he had found a beautiful white flower whose petals contained a pearl. In the dream, he took the flower and carried it to the castle, and there he was able to open each door and each and every one of the wicker baskets that contained the birds. To achieve this, he touched the door and the baskets with his white flower, freeing Florinda in the end.

The next morning, when he woke up, he immediately set out to find the flower he had dreamed of. He spent eight straight days looking for it, and on the ninth day, he found a snow-white flower that had in the middle of its petals a dewdrop the size of a pearl.

He plucked the flower with great care and made his way to the castle. He crossed the magic circle and noticed that thanks to the flower, nothing bad was happening to him, and continued walking until he reached the door without being hindered by anything. Emboldened by this discovery, Joel touched the door with the flower, and immediately the door opened.

He entered the castle and saw a gloomy courtyard, and stood in the middle, listening to the birdsong, which came to him very clearly. When he heard the song of the sweet complaint of the turtledove again, his sorrows turned into joy because, through the song, what he now perceived was the pleasant and sweet melody of the song of an ancient Greek goddess called Nana Mouskori. Listening to this song turned all sorrow into joy and gave him the desire to live forever. The song had the power to instill in the listener an overflowing candor of youth that intoned their soul and gave them the desire to want to live forever.

Guided by this song, he went through various rooms until he found himself in a very large room where there were seven thousand baskets, each of them containing a bird.

Joel entered the huge room as the witch was feeding them. Upon seeing him, the witch stopped what she was doing, turned, and began to scream and spit furiously at the young man. She was uttering dreadful curses, and venomous and loathsome spittle shot forth from between her wrinkled lips, but none of it reached Joel, and though the old hag tried, she failed to scratch him with those long, claw-sharp fingernails of hers.

He did not pay the slightest attention to these attacks but released the birds one after the other, all the while wondering how he was going to find Florinda amid the many baskets. Suddenly, he noticed that the witch had picked up a basket and was walking away with it towards the door.

Joel ran across the room with all his might, touched the basket with his white flower, and the basket burst open. He then touched the witch with the flower, and suddenly all her evil powers vanished. And there stood Florinda, as beautiful as ever. She put her arms around him and pulled him into a warm embrace. The long time that had passed had in no way affected her beauty, nor had it made her any older.

Joel set all the other birds free. Besides Florinda, he too was amazed to see how the birds in the castle turned into the beautiful maidens that had disappeared in the community; like the stone statues surrounding the castle, they regained their human form and returned to their community to the jubilant amazement of their families. After that, they never again feared as they quietly enjoyed the beauty of the forest on a summer evening.

Eventually, he and Florinda returned home, where they soon married and lived happily for the rest of their lives.

Chapter 18

Little Brother and Little Sister

Little Brother took Little Sister by the hand.

"Listen," he whispered, "since mother died, we haven't been happy for a moment. Our stepmother spanks us every day, and her one-eyed daughter kicks us away whenever we try to get close. Besides, they only feed us stale crumbs of dry bread. The dog that lies under the table eats better than we do. Many times, he is offered a piece of tasty meat. God knows mother would not consent to all this happening to us if she could see it. Let's get out of here together; the world is big, and it's waiting for us. We wouldn't live any worse, and we wouldn't have to live like tramps."

Little Sister nodded her head, for all that Little Brother had said was true. They waited until they saw their stepmother nod off, and then they left the house, quietly closing the door behind them. After walking all day through meadows and fields and through pastures and stony places, it began to rain, and Little Sister said:

"God has begun to weep, and our hearts weep with him."

At nightfall, they came to a forest. They were so tired and hungry and so afraid of the darkness that was beginning to close in around them that they were unable to do anything but climb up the hollow trunk of a tree and fall asleep.

When they awoke the next morning, the sun was already shining and illuminating the inside of the tree. Little Brother said:

"Wake up, sister! The sun is shining, the weather is fine, and I'm very thirsty. I think I hear the sound of a stream. Come on, let's go and drink!" Little Sister woke up, and, holding hands, they went in search of the stream they heard running through the trees.

Unbeknownst to them, their stepmother was a witch. She was able to see with her eyelids closed and was watching the children as they tiptoed away and left the house. She went out after them, crawling as witches often do, with her whole body glued to the ground, and before returning home in the same way, she cast a spell and bewitched all the streams in the forest.

The two children soon found the stream that's waters they had heard running and saw the cool water sparkling and leaping over the stones. It was so inviting that they both knelt to drink from the stream.

But Little Sister had learned to understand what the waters of the brooks were saying as they flowed down the stream, and she understood what the brook was telling them. When Little Brother was about to put the water to his lips that he had collected in his palms, she exclaimed:

"Don't drink it! This stream is bewitched. Whoever tastes its water will turn into a tiger. Leave the water! Leave it! If you don't, you'll tear me to pieces!"

Although he was very thirsty, her brother obeyed her. They started walking again and soon found another stream. This time she was the first to kneel on the bank and bent her head to hear clearly.

"No, we can't drink this water either!" she said. "I heard it say that whoever drinks this water will turn into a wolf. I fear our stepmother has cursed it."

"And as thirsty as I am!" he exclaimed.

"If you were to become a wolf, you would eat me in a few moments."

"I promise I won't eat you!"

"Wolves forget their promises. There must be a stream around here that she hasn't cursed. Let's keep looking."

It did not take them long to find a third stream. Little Sister went ahead and crouched down by the water and heard it say:

"Whoever drinks of my waters will become a deer."

Little Sister turned to her brother to explain, but this time it was too late. The poor young boy was so thirsty that he threw himself into the long stream and dipped his face in the water. At once, his face changed, growing longer and covered with fine hair, and his limbs changed into that of a deer. Then he staggered awkwardly on his legs, now a little fawn.

She also noticed that the animal was looking around very nervously as if it was about to run away, so she put her arms around its neck and hugged it.

"It's me, little brother, it's your little sister! Don't run away, because if you leave, we'll never meet again! Poor little brother, what have you done?" She began to cry, and her little brother cried too, until she began to recover little by little and said:

"Stop crying, my precious fawn. I will never, ever leave you. Come on, let's try to make the best of this situation."

Using the golden garter she was wearing, Little Sister looped it around the fawn's neck and then took a few reeds, plaited them together, and made a leash with which she fastened the garter. She began to walk deeper into the forest, leading the fawn behind her.

After walking a long way, they reached a clearing where there was a small house. Little Sister stopped and looked around first. It was quiet. The garden surrounding the cottage was well-kept, and the front door was open.

"Is anyone home?" cried Little Sister.

There was no response. She gave the fawn a gentle tug, and they both went inside and found that it was the cleanest and prettiest little house they had ever seen. Their stepmother didn't like to take care of their house, so it was always cold and dirty. This place, unlike their home, was beautiful.

"Do you know what we are going to do? We'll take care of this house as best we know how, and we'll always keep it clean and tidy for whoever owns it. And then they won't mind if we stay here."

She constantly talked to the fawn, and he understood her very well and obeyed her. She would sometimes say to him:

"Don't eat the plants in the garden, and if you feel like peeing or doing anything else, go out of the house."

She prepared a bed for her with fresh moss and leaves next to the hearth. Every morning, she went out to forage for food like berries, wild fruits, and sweet roots for herself. There were carrots and cabbages in the garden, and she also gathered a lot of fresh grass for the fawn, who enjoyed eating out of her hand. The fawn liked to play around her, and in the evening, after Little Sister had washed and said her prayers, she would lie down and rest her head on the fawn. If her brother hadn't turned into a fawn, that would have been a perfect life.

They lived this way for some time. But it happened that one day the king organized a great hunt in the forest. The trees resounded with the sound of hunting horns, the barking of dogs, and the excited cries of the hunters. The fawn pricked up its ears stiffly, eager to take part in the hunt.

"Let me go, sister! I'd give anything to participate too!"

So passionate was his pleading that, at last, she yielded.

"Now then," she said as she opened the door for him, "don't forget to come home after dark. I'll keep the door locked to get rid of the hunters, in case they go mad as usual. So, when you come back, let me know it's you. Knock on the door and say, 'Little sister, your brother has come home.' Because if you don't say that, I won't open the door."

The fawn took off like a bolt of lightning and bounded into the thicket of the forest. He had never felt so good, happy, and free. The hunters spotted him and began to chase him, but they were unable to catch him. Every time they approached him, and they were convinced that this time he would not escape, the deer would jump fast and disappear into the thicket. In the evening, he ran to the cottage and knocked on the door.

"Sister, your brother has returned!"

His little sister opened the door, and the fawn trotted in happily and began to tell her what had happened during the hunt. And then he slept soundly all night.

When dawn broke, and he heard the music of hunting horns in the distance, he could not resist the temptation.

"Please, Sister, I beg you, open the door! If I don't go to the forest and take part in the hunt, I'll die of grief!"

Though not very convinced, Little Sister opened the door and said:

"And don't forget the password when you come back!"

Without even bothering to answer, the fawn trotted off on its way to the hunt. When the king and the hunters who accompanied him saw the fawn with the golden collar, they immediately set off in pursuit of it. Crossing fields of ferns and brambles, through thickets and clearings, the fawn spent the whole day running and driving the hunters crazy as they spent hours in pursuit of it. On several occasions, they almost caught up with him, and when the sun was already setting, he was wounded in the leg with a shot from a shotgun. Because of that, he was no longer running as fast as before, and

one of the hunters managed to follow his trail, went after him, and saw him arrive at the little house, knock on the door, and utter the words:
"Sister, your brother is back!"

Not long after, the hunter saw the door open, and a girl let the fawn in and closed the door behind him. And the hunter went back to where the king was and told him all about it.

"Is that so?" the king asked. "Then we will hunt him harder tomorrow."

Little Sister was very frightened when she saw the deer's wound. She washed away the blood that stained his hoof and prepared a bundle of healing herbs to put on the wound. It was not a serious wound, and the next morning, when the fawn awoke, he had forgotten all about it. And for the third time, he begged to be allowed to leave.

"Sister, I can't tell you how much I love hunting! If I don't go out again, I'm going to go crazy!"

His little sister began to sob:

"Yesterday you were wounded," she said through her tears, "and today they will kill you, and I will be left all alone in the middle of these wild woods. Think of that! I'll have no one by my side! I can't let you go. I can't!"

"Then I'll die here, right under your nose. When I hear the notes of the hunting horn, every part of my body starts to jump for joy. Sister, I won't resist the desire to leave! Let me go, I beg you!"

She was unable to refuse any longer in the face of the intensity of those pleas, and with her heart in a fist, she finally opened the door. Without looking back, the fawn bound out of the house and vanished into the forest.

Meanwhile, the king had ordered the hunters not to cause the slightest harm to the fawn with the golden collar.

"He who spots him, let him raise his gun to the sky and hold the dogs. I offer ten gold trollers to the one who spots him first!"

They chased the deer through the forest and throughout the whole day, and when the sun was setting, the king called the hunter who had told him the story and said:

"I want you to take me to that little house. If we can't catch him in the woods, we'll catch him some other way. What was the phrase you heard him say?"

The hunter repeated the words to the king. When they reached the cottage, the king knocked on the door and said:

“Sister, your brother has returned!”

The door opened instantly. The king entered and found standing at the door the most beautiful girl he had ever seen in his life. The girl was frightened because she was waiting for the fawn, and instead of him, a stranger had entered the cottage, but the man wore a golden crown on his head and smiled kindly at her. Then he reached forward and took the girl's hand.

“Will you come to the palace with me and be a princess in my palace?” he asked.

“Of course!” replied Little Sister. “But my fawn will have to come with me. If he doesn't come with me, I can't accept your offer.”

“Of course. He can also come with you," said the king. “He will live as long as you, and he will never want for anything.”

And just as he uttered these words, the deer came bounding in and entered the little house. Little Sister took hold of his golden collar and tied him up with a rope of plaited reeds.

By mutual agreement, the girl agreed to go with the king. The king made the girl get on the back of his horse, and they returned to the palace, and the fawn trotted very proudly, after his little sister and the king.

After returning to his palace, the king ordered that the girl be cared for and educated with all due care, for she was to be the princess who would later marry his only son, the prince of the palace when he was a young man.

As time passed, the king organized the most lavish wedding of his reign, a celebration designed for his son and the princess, with all the guests of honor from all his neighboring kingdoms showering the new royal couple with the most luxurious gifts befitting their royal status.

When the father became an old man, he abdicated his throne and crowned his only son and the princess as king and queen, who lived happily for a long time.

As for his little brother, the deer, from the moment of his arrival at the palace, he was allowed to play all over the palace garden, and a host of servants were put at his service. A groom oversaw providing him with grass, the valet with the hunting horn took care of his hooves, and the maid with the golden brush was given the task of combing his hair thoroughly every evening before he went to bed, and she would shoo away any flies and get rid of ticks and lice that might have gotten stuck in his fur. So, they were all very happy until they were discovered by the witch who oppressed them when they were children.

Well, during all this time, the wicked stepmother was convinced that Little Sister and Little Brother had been the prey of the vermin. But when she read in the newspaper that Little Sister was the new queen and that her daily companion was a deer, she immediately deduced what had happened.

"That wretched boy must have drunk water from the stream where I put the evil spell that turned whoever drank into a deer!" she said to her daughter.

"It's not fair that she should be queen instead of me," her daughter whined.

"Stop whining," said the mother, "When the time comes, you will become what you deserve."

A long time passed, and the queen gave birth to a very handsome boy. That day, as usual, the king went hunting. The witch and her daughter entered the palace disguised as ladies-in-waiting and managed to make their way into the queen's chambers.

"Get ready, your majesty," said the witch to the queen, who was very weak and exhausted in bed. "Your bath is ready. After taking it, you will feel much better. Come with us!"

They took her to a giant pot filled with bathwater and put her inside. Then they lit a big fire under the pot, so big that the queen began to feel asphyxiation from so much smoke. So that their crime would remain hidden from everyone's eyes, they used magic to make the door of the place where the queen was in the pot disappear, and they hung a tapestry to hide that place.

"Now you must get into her bed," said the stepmother to her daughter, and as soon as the girl got into the bed, the witch enchanted her so that she looked exactly like the queen. But there was one thing she could not fix—her daughter's missing eye.

She said, "Put that side of your face on the pillow, and if anyone speaks to you, just mumble."

When the king returned to the palace that night and was told that he had had a son, he was happy. He went up to his beloved wife's bedroom and was about to open the curtains to see how she was doing when the witch, who had disguised herself as a lady-in-waiting, said:

"Don't open them, your Majesty! Leave the curtains closed, and don't open them under any pretext! The queen needs to rest, and no one must disturb her!"

The king tiptoed around the room and retired to his chambers, so he did not discover that in the bed lay a false queen.

That night the deer by no means wanted to sleep in the stable, where he usually did. He climbed the stairs and made his way to the room where the newborn slept, refusing to leave. He could not give any kind of explanation, for since the death of the queen, he had lost the gift of speech. So, he merely lay down by the cradle and went to sleep.

When midnight came, the maiden who slept in that room suddenly awoke and saw the queen coming in there, and it seemed to her that she was soaked from head to foot as if she had just come out of the bath. The queen bent over the cradle, kissed the little one, and then caressed the deer and crooned:

How is my little one? And how is my fawn?

I'll come back another two times, and no one will ever see me again.

And having said that, she left.

The maid was so frightened that she dared not tell anyone. She was sure that the queen had been lying in bed, recovering from childbirth.

But the next night, the same thing happened again, only this time the queen seemed to be covered with small flames, and she said:

How is my little one? And how is my fawn?

I will come back once more, then no one will ever see me again.

The maid thought she should tell the king. So, the next night, they both waited in the newborn's room, and at midnight, the queen appeared there again. This time she was enveloped in a thick cloud of black smoke.

"Oh, God, what is this?" cried the king.

The queen ignored him and, approaching the boy and the deer as she had done before, she said:

How is my little one? And how is my fawn?

I must leave now, and no one will ever see me again.

This time the king tried to embrace her, but she disappeared into a cloud of smoke, slipped out of his embrace, and melted into thin air.

The deer tugged at the king's sleeve and dragged him to the place where a tapestry hung. Then he tugged at the tapestry until it fell to the ground and hit the wall with its horns. The king understood what he meant and ordered his servants to tear down the wall. With all that noise, the false queen got out of bed and tiptoed away without anyone noticing her. Once the wall was torn down, they discovered on the other side the bath, which was completely blackened with soot, and inside the pot, they found the body of the queen, who now looked very pale.

"My wife, my beloved wife!" exclaimed the king.

He stooped to embrace her, and by the grace of God, the queen was restored to life. She told him at once of the horrible crime that had been committed against her, and the king sent the swiftest of his messengers to the palace gate just in time to inform the guards that they were to arrest the witch and her daughter when they caught them trying to escape.

Both women were brought before the king, and the sentence was passed: the daughter was condemned to be taken to the forest and left there to be eaten by vermin, and the witch was condemned to die at the stake. As soon as the old woman was reduced to ashes, her spell lost all its power, and the deer was transformed into Little Brother. The queen then ordered the best treatment and honors for her brother, who, despite the hardships and misfortunes they had to confront, had helped her face life with courage.

After the destruction of the witch's spell, the king and queen became the most beloved and acclaimed rulers of all time. Little Brother and Little Sister, now queen, lived happily together for the rest of their lives.